The world is but a canvas to our imagination.
—HENRY DAVID THOREAU

THE DEVIL'S FORK

BILL WITTLIFF

The Devil's Fork

Illustrated by EDWARD CAREY

University of Texas Press, *Austin*

Requests for permission to reproduce material
from this work should be sent to:
    Permissions
    University of Texas Press
    P.O. Box 7819
    Austin, TX 78713-7819
    utpress.utexas.edu/rp-form

The paper used in this book meets the minimum
requirements of ANSI/NISO Z39.48-1992 (R1997)
(Permanence of Paper). ∞

LIBRARY OF CONGRESS CATALOGING-IN-PUBLICATION DATA
Names: Wittliff, William D., author. | Carey, Edward, 1970–, illustrator.
Title: The devil's fork / Bill Wittliff ; illustrated by Edward Carey.
Description: First edition. | Austin : University of Texas Press, 2018.
Identifiers: LCCN 2018003964
ISBN 978-1-4773-1758-7 (cloth : alk. paper)
ISBN 978-1-4773-1759-4 (library e-book)
ISBN 978-1-4773-1760-0 (nonlibrary e-book)
Subjects: LCSH: Texas—Fiction. | Families—Texas—Fiction.
Classification: LCC PS3573.I933 D42 2018 | DDC 813/.54—dc23
LC record available at https://lccn.loc.gov/2018003964

doi:10.7560/317587

For My Brother

JIM

And For My Pals

KATE BREAKEY

PAT & KEITH CARTER

THE DEVIL'S FORK

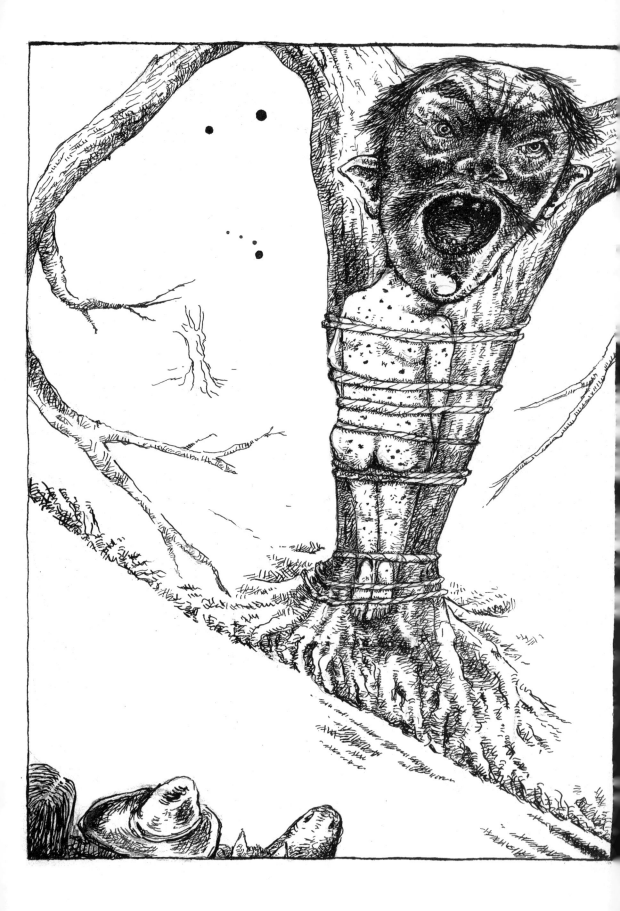

THE FIRST THING O'JEFFEY SAID

after she passed over, Papa said, was they was gonna hang my o'Amigo Calley Pearsall out there in front a'the Alamo down in San Antoneya come Saturday Noon and if I was gonna stop it I better Light a Shuck and Get on over there. And I mean Right Now, she said. So, he said, me and Annie and o'Fritz jumped up on Sister and I give her my heels and a'way we did go.

OH LISTEN HERE,

Papa said, Sister Run and she Run and she Run and they wadn't no stopping her til we was to the Guadaloop River and all four a'us down on our knees a'getting us a drink a'Water. I never seen a'Horse with such Bottom as Sister got have you I said and Annie said No and I bet they's some thing over yonder you ain't never seen neither then pointed her finger cross the River to where a Neckid Man was tied to a tree with his o'Bare Hiney just a'Shining. You all right Mister I hollered, Papa said, and the Neckid Man said some thing back but we couldn't hear what it was. We better go see, Annie said, and her and Fritz went a'wading on cross. Just hang on there a minute Annie, Papa said, that Man ain't got his Pants on but she didn't pay me no mine like almost always so I grabbed the Blanket off my Momma's Mexkin Saddle and waded on cross my self and now I seen that Neckid Man's Belongings was scattered all round over there by where his little Horse Cart was a'setting with out no Horse. Looks like somebody stole your Horse huh Mister I said, Papa said, and throwed my Blanket over him to where couldn't me or Annie or Any Body see nothing. Oh, Papa said, he had big Red Pecks all over him where the Bugs and whatnot been a'eating on him and he was Red from a Sun Bath too. Them SonsaBitches, the man said, Stole my Mule and ever thing else they could run off with. And when he said that, Papa said, he give a Mean Look had Thunder and Lightning in it and spit a Gob at poor o'Fritz,

I bet they's some thing over yonder
you ain't never seen neither . . .

/

who hadn't never done nothing to him in his Life. You better keep that little Piss Ant of a Dog a'way from me fore I ty a Rock on him and throw him in the River the Man said. And you better be careful what you say Mister, Annie said, or we might just have to sic him on you for your Bad Manners. But, Papa said, we went on and untied him any how and he dropped to the ground like a'Sack a'Pataters. God dam that hurt he said. Now gimme a'Hand here I got to get on to San Antoneya and find my Little Brother Johnny. We got to get on to San Antoneya ourself, Papa said, fore they Hang our o'Amigo Calley Pearsall out there in front a'the Alamo at Saturday Noon. That ain't til Day after Tomorra, Annie said, Don't Worry we'll get there in time. What'd your friend do to earn him his Hanging, the Man said. He lost his Temper and kilt a Man out on the Street is all we been tole, Papa said. Yes Sir an Eye for an Eye, the Man said. That's God's Law and I'm sorry but they just ain't nothing you can do bout it is they. No Sir if I was you he said I believe I'd just go on back Home fore it gets too Dark to see. Then, Papa said, he tried to stand up but went down on his poor o'red Hiney a'gain in sted. God dam that hurt he said. You hurting all over ain't you Mister, Annie said. Oh you don't have to worry bout me, the Man said, I been a'Hurting pretty much all my Life. Yall just go on now. But, Papa said, I Knowed and Annie Knowed we wadn't never gonna just go off and leave Somebody like that where some o'Wild Animal might come a'long and eat him up or them Ruffians robbed him might come back and finish they Job on him. We ain't a'going off and just leave you Mister I said, Papa said, and Annie said Yes Sir that's right Mister Who ever you are. Pugh, the Man said, Simon Pugh then he chunked a Rock at o'Fritz just to be Mean but o'Fritz side stepped a'side and went Heh Heh Heh.

*M*E AND ANNIE
went over there and waded Sister on cross, Papa said, then hitched her to o'Simon Pugh's little wagon and helped him up. How's that Leg Mister Pugh, Annie said, and he said Couldn't be no better but, Papa said, we could tell it was a'hurting him same as all them Bug Bites ever wheres else was too. We gonna have to take you to Doctor Herff, Annie said. He's the best they is in San Antoneya. Yes Sir, Mister Pugh said, I'll take me a German

2

Doctor any day a'the week. They so Hard Headed they don't hardly never let you die on em. But a Irish Doctor, he said, a Irish Doctor just gonna Drink Drink Drink til he falls over on you and breaks you other Leg. Oh I seen that happen many the time up in the Camps where a Irish Doctor is bout all they can get. What Camps you talking bout, Papa said, you wadn't in Some Body's Army was you. The Camps I'm talking bout was up there in Colarada you know where that is he said. Yes Sir some wheres up yonder ain't it I said, Papa said. That's where you been a'living huh Mister Pugh, Annie said. Yep up til some o'Mountain Lion et my Daddy for Breakfast one morning and I was gone on down the Road by Dark. What bout your Momma, Annie said. You didn't just go off and leave her did you. No, he said, Momma run off her self here bout ten twenty years ago. Colarada didn't suit her huh, Annie said. No Colarada suited her fine, he said, it was my o'Daddy didn't suit her so she blowed him a Kiss and went on off down the Road. Yall can talk bout it all you want, Papa said, but me and Fritz gotta get on to San Antoneya. Where you gonna be so I can find you, Annie said. First place we a'going is to the Jail House, he said, then I'm gonna have to Stop em from hanging o'Calley don't matter a Lick what it is I got to do. You go on, Annie said, we'll catch up with you in San Antoneya. So, Papa said, I give Sister a Hug round her neck to say Adios and she give me a Nuzzle on my Ear and then me and o'Fritz took off a'Trotting cross the Country on our own Feet to get to San Antoneya quick's we could and then I heared Annie hollering Be Careful Be Careful back behind me and, he said, I raised my John B Stetson Hat up off my Head to say Yes Annie I hear you and we kep on a'going.

*T*URNED OUT WE didn't have near the Bottom o'Sister had, Papa said, and wadn't but maybe three four hours a'Trotting cross the Country like that and me and o'Fritz was both give out and had to set down and take us a Rest then get a'drink a'Water at this little Creek we come to. Course it was Night by now, he said, and they was Owls a'Hooting and Coyotes a'Yipping ever wheres you listened and o'Fritz tried to yip back but all that come out was a'little Squeek. They gonna come get you for making fun of em like that if you ain't careful Fritz I said but then o'Fritz heared some thing else and hushed up and then

I heared it too, Papa said, and what it was was some Men just a'Whooping and a'Hollering and a'Carrying on out there in the Dark some wheres cross the Creek. I bet they Drunk on some thing ain't they I said, Papa said, then me and Fritz crossed on over the Creek and went to sneaking through the Woods to where all that Whooping and Hollering was a'coming from and Oh, he said, they was two men a'Dancing round they Camp Fire and a'Falling down ever other step they took and a'Laughing bout it ever time. They Drunk on some thing sure nough ain't they Fritz I said and o'Fritz give me one a'his Grins and went Heh Heh Heh. Oh and then, Papa said, they was a'big He a'He a'He HawHaw and we looked over there and they was this o'Mule a'standing there by two saddled up Horses and I figgured for sure that was Mister Pugh's o'Mule and these two Fool Drunk Dancers here is the ones stole him and tyed poor o'Mister Pugh Neckid to that Tree so the Bugs and what all could get him. These is two Bad Men we got here Fritz I said, Papa said, and we got to get on outta here quick's we can. But then, Papa said, it come to me we could get to San Antoneya a'lot quicker if we was a'riding Mister Pugh's o'Mule and not only that but I could give him back to Mister Pugh once we was all back together again in San Antoneya. Well I reckon we just borned Lucky wadn't we huh Fritz I said then we sneaked over there and untyed Mister Pugh's Mule and then just for Mean-ness for what they done to Mister Pugh I untyed they Horses too so they could run off some wheres in the Dark and be Hard to find. Then I got up on that o'Mule and Fritz jumped up on there with me and fore I could even show him which way to go Why that o'Mule turned and went a'walking off toward San Antoneya and I thought Oh Boy Hidy this is one smart o'Mule we got here ain't it He knows where we a'wanting to go without me ever even having to tell him.

I WAITED TIL WE WAS OUT A'HEARING a'them Two Robbers, Papa said, then give that o'Mule a'touch a'my Heels to get on outta there but No, he said, that o'Mule had his own Notion bout it and stuck to his own Pace no matter how much Heel I give him. This is where that o'saying Stubborn as a Mule comes from ain't it Fritz I said but o'Fritz was already to sleep in my lap and didn't pay me no mine. Yes Sir you

go on and get you some sleep Fritz I said, Papa said, Don't worry I'll keep a
Eye out so the Inyins don't get you but No he didn't pay no attention to my
Joke neither and I got to thinking bout my o'Amigo Calley Pearsall and what
I might have to do to save him from his Hanging and Oh I wished I had me a
Pistol or two and some Bullets. And after that, Papa said, I wished o'Genral
Sam Houston was a'riding here long side me with bout a'hunderd a'his best
Soldier Boys with they Guns and Knives ready. What you want us to do
Mister, Genral Houston said, and I said First thing Genral is I don't want no
Harm to come to Mister Calley Pearsall if you can help it and o'Genral Hous-
ton hollered at his Texican Boys Yall hear that Boys he don't want no Harm
to come to Mister Calley Pearsall and then, Papa said, his Boys give a salute
and pulled they Pistols and Knives out they Pants and hollered back Don't
worry bout it Genral they ain't no Harm gonna come to Mister Calley Pearsall long as we got some thing to say bout it. Oh and then they Drummer
Boys started a'Drumming they Drums and they Flag Boys started a'Waving
they Flags and they Horses started a'Stomping they feet and then o'Genral
Houston turned and give me a Salute and said Lead On Lead On we right
here behind you Mister and so, Papa said, I pointed my Arm to San Antoneya
and hollered Charge Charge Charge and Genral Houston and all his Soldier
Boys come a'Charging long behind me just a'Hollering and a'Shooting they
Guns off in ever which Direction to show they wadn't nobody in the World
gonna Hang my o'Amigo Calley Pearsall and Oh the Crowd all long the Road
went to Whooping and Cheering and Throwing they Hats up in the Air to
say Hoo Ray Hoo Ray Hoo Ray for o'Calley Pearsall but we didn't have no
time for that and run on pass em but, Papa said, I reckon it was all that
Whooping and Cheering waked me up just when the Sun come a'Shining up
over the Hill cause I looked round and seen Oh here we are in San Antoneya
where we was a'Going in the First Place.

O'FRITZ WAKED UP
bout that time too, Papa said, then got him a sniff a'Some thing or other
in the Air and took off a'running down the Street and round the Corner
and when I got down there to see where he went, he said, Why there he
was a'setting on the Board Walk out there in front a'the Jail House where

o'Possum and Mister Loonie and that poor Little o'One Eyed Bear was all just a'Crying they Hearts out and Howling at the Moon. What's wrong with yall to be Carrying on like this I said, Papa said, but I knowed it was cause they didn't want Mister Pearsall to Hang no moren I did. Then, he said, I seen they was all tyed to the Hitching Rail and couldn't go no wheres even if they wanted to and I said who was it so Mean to ty yall to the Hitching Rail like this and a Voice come up behind me and said Well it was Sheriff Highschoote his self done it and what the god dam Hell you a'doing with his Mule any how. I looked round then, Papa said, and there was the Deputy Sheriff a'standing there with his Pistol a'pointing at me. I didn't do nothing I said, Papa said. Where's Sheriff Highschoote the Deputy said. Well if this is his Mule here, Papa said, the last I seen a'him he was a'Dancing round in the Woods with some other Fella but I thought they was some body else. You sure you didn't steal the Sheriff's Mule, the Deputy said. No Sir, Papa said, I didn't even know him that much. Well where is he then, the Deputy said. I don't have no Idear, Papa said. You know we hang a Man for stealing a Mule sames we do a Man for stealing a Horse he said. I didn't steal the Sheriff's Mule, Papa said. I thought the one I stole was the one them two Other Men stole off Mister Pugh and I was just trying to set it right and get a ride to San Antoneya both at the same time. Oh the Deputy give me a poke in my Belly with his pistol then and said So you admitting to be a Mule Theif then ain't you. Yes Sir I admit I stole the Mule them Robbers stole off Mister Pugh, Papa said, but No Sir I didn't never steal Sheriff Highschoote's Mule even if I come a'riding in to Town on him. If I'd a'knowed it was the Sheriff's Mule why I'd a'just walked to San Antoneya on my own two Feet. Well we just gonna have to wait and see what the Judge got to say bout this, the Deputy said. Yes Sir, Papa said, Well let's go talk to the Judge right now then. We can't, the Deputy said. He's with the Sheriff. Meantime, he said, I got just the Place for you to wait then he give me a push on in the Jail House.

*F*IRST THING I SEEN when I come in the Jail House was Pela Rosa a'holding Hands with o'Calley through the Bars but, he said, course o'Calley couldn't hardly see me cause his eyes was so swole up from a'Bad Whupping some body give him. Oh

First thing I seen when I come in the Jail House was Pela Rosa a'holding Hands with o'Calley through the Bars . . .

that Copper Taste come up in my mouth then like always when some thing riled me. Who done that to you Mister Pearsall I said, Papa said. Sheriff Highschoote but don't worry bout it, Calley said, me and you might a'done the same thing to him if the Sheriff'd a'killed our Little Brother like I did his. Why'd you go and do that, Papa said. I didn't mean to, Calley said, but I lost my temper and took the Devil's Fork. He was Poking that o'Loonie and Possum and that poor Little o'One Eyed Bear with a Sharp Stick and wouldn't quit it, Pela Rosa said, and Oh them poor Creatures was just a'Hollering and a'Crying and a'Hugging on each other to save they self but No the Sheriff's Little Brother wouldn't quit and we heared em Crying from up in Senyora Garza's Place and and and And then, Calley said, Why I come down here and seen that Son of a Bitch a'poking them poor Creatures like that and I said Quit It Mister Quit It Right Now or I'm gonna know the Reason Why but No he was just a'Laughing and having him a'Time of it and didn't pay me no mine So I stepped down off the Board Walk and tole him he was bout to get him a Good Whupping his self if he didn't Quit It but No he was just having him too much Fun to Quit It so, he said, I lost my temper and give him a Knock on his Head with my o'Pistola to pay attention but No it Killed him deadern a god dam Anvil even if I didn't mean it to. That's what happens when you make a Bad Decision and take the Devil's Fork, he said, sometimes you do some thing you can't never get back from. Well he had it coming if you ask me, Pela Rosa said, them poor Creatures didn't do nothing to him. Don't you worry Mister Pearsall, I said, I ain't gonna let no body Hang you but I was bout to Cry when I said it cause I didn't have no Idea how in the World I was gonna do that. Then Pela started Crying and give me a tight Hug to where I couldn't hardly breathe and Calley reached through the Bars and put his Hand on my Shoulder. You go on Amigo, he said, but Remember me in you Old Age for all the Good Times we had when we was Wild and Free and a'Riding round the Country together without a'Care in the World. Oh and then I did Cry, Papa said, but right then the Deputy come back in from out side and said Well here's a Surprise the Judge and Sheriff Highschoote both just got back in Town and then, Papa said, he pushed the Door wide open for us to see and what we Seen, he said, was bout half the Town follering Mister Pugh and Annie down the street in they Wagon and in the back was two Dead Bodies and Oh I seen right a'way they was the two

Drunk Men me and o'Fritz come up on a'Dancing round they Camp Fire last night. Well Fritz I said, Papa said, Looks like they Dancing Days is over ain't they.

*T*HEN, Papa said, when the Town went to unloading the Dead Bodies why that o'Loonie seen Mister Pugh climbing off the Wagon and just went to Hollering and a'Flapping his little Arms like some o'Bird you might a'seen some wheres. Who you Hollering at Boy, Mister Pugh said then of a sudden he seen it was his Long Lost Little Brother he been a'looking for and his eyes went to raining Tears. Johnny, he said, Johnny is that You. Is that You. Oh and then o'Johnny went to Hollering some more and a'Flapping his Arms and a'trying to go to his Big Brother but some Man reached his foot out to Trip him and poor o'Johnny went down on his Face but Oh Listen here Mister Pugh threw the blanket off his neckid self and went after that Man like some o'Panther. Oh he hit him and he hit him and he kicked him and he kicked him and then he picked up a big Rock off the Street and went to hitting him in the Mouth with it til that Man didn't have not even one Tooth left in his Head. And Oh, Papa said, the Town drawed way back cause they never seen a Neckid Man throw such a Fit in all they Life. Oh and then, he said, Mister Pugh run over there to give his Little Brother Johnny a'Hello and they both went to hugging on each other and just a'Crying bout it. And a'course o'Possum and that Little o'One Eyed Bear was both a'Hollering too and trying to run over there but No they was both tyed to the Board Walk and couldn't get a'loose So, Papa said, I reached down there and undid the Knot and Oh now both of em run down there and jumped on Mister Pugh and Johnny and then even o'Fritz run down there and jumped on too and they all went down in a Pile and Oh you never seen such Crying and Howling and Happyness in all you Life, Papa said, but then the next thing was Annie come a'Running up to me just a'Crying and said I been Worried sick bout you. I'm alright Annie, Papa said, I'm getting long just fine. Maybe you think you are, the Deputy said, but No Sir you ain't not by a Long Shot. Well now why ain't he, Annie said. Cause some body got to answer for Murdering the Judge and the Sheriff that's why, the Deputy said. Well you don't think for one minute he done it do you, Annie said, you ain't that stupid are you Mister. Well he come a'riding in here on the Sheriff's Mule this morning the Deputy said, I reckon that tells you some thing bout who Murdered em don't it And don't call me Mister while you at it, he said, I'm Deputy Pahmeyer and I reckon I'm the Sheriff round here from now on ain't I. Oh and then, Papa said, he looked over and give o'Dead Sheriff Highschoote a'little Grin bout it and hiked his Pants up like he had him a Job to do and was gonna do it come Hell or High Water didn't matter a'Lick which one come first. Then, Papa said, he put his Hand on his Pistol there in his Belt and give the People a Look all a'round like You better not Mess with me Mister.

 $\mathscr{B}$ UT RIGHT THEN, Papa said, Mister Pugh said Hey and we all looked over there to where Mister Pugh was a'helping his Little Brother Johnny take his shirt off. Hey What, Deputy Pahmeyer said. You take your Little o'Brother and go on now. No Sir I ain't a'going no wheres Not til some body tells me what Son of a Bitch round here been a'Poking my Little Brother with a'Pointy Stick or some thing. And then, Papa said, Mister Pugh pulled Johnny's shirt back to show bout a hunderd Bloody Red Pock Marks all up and down Johnny's body where some body sure nough been a'Poking him with a Pointy Stick and Oh you could tell Mister Pugh was Mad Mad Mad bout it and wadn't just gonna let it go neither. You git on, Deputy Pahmeyer said, I ain't got time to Fool with you now. It must a'been the Sheriff's Little Brother who was a'poking him, Papa said, and then Mister Pearsall come out and give him a Lick with his big o'Pistola for it and it accidentally kilt him deadern a'Anvil. Yes Sir and now we gonna Hang him for it tomorra Noon out there front a'the Alamo where ever body wants to can watch, the Deputy said, then give o'Pugh a Look and said Now git on like I tole you or you gonna be setting in a cell with this Boy here. Mister Pugh give him a Look that'd burn a Hole in a Saddle Blanket then and said Ain't no Boy done this to the Judge or Sheriff neither one and wadn't just one Man done it neither. Look a'here, he said then went to pointing at all the different Bullet Holes in they bodies with his Finger. This One here is from a Pistol and this One and this

One and that One over there is too But this One here and that One there and them other two down there by the Judge's Privates is all from a big gun a'some kind or other. I guess you was just borned a Idjit not to a'seen that, huh, Deputy. I seen ever thing, Deputy Pahmeyer said, Don't go Chiding me. Yes Sir I believe ever word you say, Mister Pugh said. Now take me to this Mister Calley Pearsall yall been a'talking bout, he said. I wanna shake his Hand for what he done for my Little Brother Johnny. Then after that, he said, I'm gonna buy me and Johnny a'new suit a'Clothes.

MISTER PEARSALL I'M SIMON PUGH

Mister Pugh said when we got in the Jail House, Papa said, and I wanna shake your Hand for what I hear you done for my Little Brother Johnny when the Sheriff's Little Brother was a'Poking him with that Pointy Stick. Well that's how the World works ain't it, o'Calley said. One Man wants to Hang You for some thing you done while the next one wants to Shake you Hand for the same dam thing. Deputy Pahmeyer let go a little Laugh at that but Mister Pugh give him a look and he dried it right up again. You quick to Judge ain't you Deputy, Mister Pugh said, I reckon that o'Dead Sheriff out there in the Wagon was the same god dam Way wadn't he and you learned it from him. Didn't neither one a'you care a Tinker's Dam bout some body going round poking the Helpless did you. Oh, Papa said, the Deputy looked round and seen o'Johnny and Possum and that Little o'One Eyed Bear and o'Fritz too all just a'Looking at him like he was some thing smelled Bad and said I'm just the Deputy it was the Sheriff his self called the Shots round here. Him and the Judge, he said, Them two. Well I'm glad you didn't have nothing to do with it Deputy, Mister Pugh said. I might think less a'you if you did. Oh I never seen such Brass on a Man as o'Pugh had on him, Papa said, and him standing there not wearing nothing but Rags and Bug Bites. You better just leave me a'lone Mister, Deputy Pahmeyer said, I wouldn't wanna have to get on you for the way you behaving here. I don't believe you got time to get on me Deputy, Mister Pugh said, not if you planning to go catch who ever it was Murdered the Sheriff and the Judge fore they vaccate the Country. I already been planning to go catch em right after the Hang- ing tomorra so just leave me a'lone bout it Deputy Pahmeyer said but, Papa said, o'Calley seen the Deputy was scared to Death bout it and just wanted his Momma. If I was you Deputy, he said, I believe I might wait for a Posse to build fore I go a'riding off just by my self on a Trip like this. That's just Good Sense ain't it. Yes it is, the Deputy said, I been a'thinking the same Thing my self. Sides that, he said, I got to officiate at your Hanging now that ever body else could do it already been Murdered. Bout then, Papa said, Mister Pugh looked out the Door and seen Annie standing over there by his Wagon. Ain't nobody been trying to steal my Wagon have they he said. No Sir not a one, Annie said. Well let's get on over to the Store then Johnny how bout that, Mister Pugh said to his Little Brother then give me a'little Push out the Door too.

PELA AND DEPUTY PAHMEYER stayed with o'Calley in the Jail House, Papa said, while me and Annie and Mister Pugh give his Brother Johnny and the Creatures a'ride over to the Joske Brother Store in his Wagon and Oh, he said, Johnny Hollered and Laughed and Waved his little Fingers at ever body all up and down the Street when we was a'going pass em and they Laughed and Waved back. Why Johnny, Mister Pugh said, I believe ever body in town is your Friend ain't they and Oh, Papa said, Johnny bout fell over Laughing but didn't have no clear idea what bout far as I could tell. O'Johnny thinks ever thing in the World is Funny don't he Mister Pugh, Annie said. I don't reckon he thought it was much Funny that Man a'poking him with that Pointy Stick do you, Mister Pugh said. No Sir Annie said. No Sir I said too, Papa said, then I said What's gonna happen to o'Johnny when he gets too old to Beg. He ain't a'Beggar no more now, Mister Pugh said then pulled Sister to a stop in front a'the Joske Brother Store and said Come look a'here. So we went round to the back a'the wagon and Mister Pugh started a'pulling boards up off the Wagon Floor, Papa said, and under them boards was a Secret Bottom where they wadn't nothing but Sand but then, he said, o'Possum and Fritz went to digging in it and Oh of a sudden why Gold Coins come a'Bubbling up out the Sand like Little Fish and they was so many of em they bout blinded you when the Sun went a'bouncing off. I packed em in Sand like this so they wouldn't Jingle and give me a'way to Bad People on my Travels, Mister Pugh said. Then this big Grin come over his Face and he said, Good thing I did too or them two Robbers would a'stole it for sure. Your Daddy give it to you fore that o'Panther got him huh, Annie said. No my Daddy never give me or no body else nothing in his Life he said. Now you gonna just put it in the Bank huh, Papa said. Well I don't see Why Not, Mister Pugh said and give another little Grin, That's where it come out from in the First Place ain't it. Oh and then he went to Laughing bout it, Papa said, and give Johnny a little Knock on his Head and Oh then Johnny went to Laughing too and then me and Annie couldn't help it and went to Laughing too same as Fritz and Possum and that Little o'One Eyed Bear was already a'doing. That's more money'n I ever seen, Annie said. What you gonna spend it on. Well, o'Pugh said, I come to San Antoneya to spend it on Johnny for what Daddy done to him and now I'm gonna do just that but First, he said, we gotta scrape him off some and get him a Bath.

*S*O WE WENT ON DOWN TO THE BATH HOUSE, Papa said, but the Owners was Scared a'what o'Johnny looked like and didn't wanna Wash him but Mister Pugh told em if they didn't treat his Little Brother Johnny like ever other good Citizen come in here Why he was gonna go get him a Match and a Bucket a'Coal Oil and burn they whole god dam place down round they Ears and Pee on they Ashes to boot and Oh then they went to scrubbing Johnny all over with they Brushes and Washing his Hair and Face and o'Johnny liked it so much he tried to get Possum and Fritz and that Little o'One Eyed Bear in the Wash Tub with him but No they wouldn't do it so Johnny just Hollered and Laughed and Splashed water on ever body so they couldn't get him out the Tub and then Mister Pugh had to go over there and wrastle him out his self. Johnny, he said, Clean's Clean and you just Clean as a Whistle now so get on out a'that god dam Wash Tub fore I go get my o'Mule and pull you out. So Johnny got out the Tub, Papa said, then seen his self all Neckid like that in the Mirra and felt so good bout how he looked he went up and down the Bath House a'Wiggling his Stick and Hollering at ever body in they Bath Tubs to Look at it too but No they didn't want no part a'some o'Neckid Man a'Wiggling his Stick like that and throwed they Hats and Towels and whatnot at him til me and Mister

13

Pugh got his Pants back on him and went on out to the Wagon where Annie was a'waiting. Why Johnny I hardly know you, she said, you so Clean I thought you was o'Sam Houston a'going off to lead a Parade or some thing. Then next thing, Papa said, was we went over to the Joske Brother Store to buy Johnny and Mister Pugh a'new Suit a'Clothes but on the way we seen the Hanging Stand out there in front a'the Alamo where they was setting up Chairs and Benches cause that's where they was gonna Hang o'Calley Tomorra Noon and it just bout undone me to see it he said.

So WE WENT ON IN THE JOSKE STORE, Papa said, and People got out the way so Johnny could hobble on by but didn't no body say No No he can't come in here. Then a Man come out from behind the Counter and said Maybe I can help you find what you a'looking for Mister and Mister Pugh said I want the Best Suit a'Clothes you got for my Little Brother Johnny here and a Suit a'Clothes for me too and whatever these two Young People here want for they self and Look a'here, he said, then slapped some Gold Coins down on the Counter loud nough for ever body to Turn and Look. I'm gonna have to get my Taylor, the Man said. I don't believe I got any thing Ready Made gonna fit your Little Brother. Yes Sir bring your Taylor, Mister Pugh said, we don't want a'Bad Fit. I reckon this gonna be the First Suit a'Clothes o'Johnny here ever had in his Life. Oh and then, Papa said, the Man give Mister Pugh a good Look all up and down for the Rags he was a'wearing and said And you too I reckon huh Mister. You wanted to see some thing You should a'seen Mister Pugh yesterday, Annie said. Why he was tyed to a Tree with his o'Neckid Hind End a'Poking out. Well don't you worry Ma'am we gonna fix it so that don't never happen again. While yall a'getting you a'new Suit a'Clothes, Papa said, I'm going back over to the Jail House to see how o'Calley's a'doing. Aint no hurry, Mister Pugh said. Your Friend ain't a'going no wheres. I'm going with him, Annie said. Well I was gonna treat yall to some thing or other for that favor yall done me. Save o'Calley for us, Papa said. That's the only Favor I'm ever gonna want in my Life. But then here come the Taylor with his Tape Measure round his Neck and he give Johnny a Look and his Mouth went in a big O and he said Hmmm Hmmm Hmmm and Mister Pugh said You

I'm gonna have to get my Taylor, the Man said. I don't believe I got any thing Ready Made gonna fit your Little Brother.

14

can Hmmm Hmmm Hmmm all you want Mister but I don't want my Little Brother Johnny Looking like a German Sausage a'Walking down the Street when you done with him. Oh and some thing bout what he said tickled o'Johnny and he went to Hollering and Laughing bout it and then Pretty soon some other People in there couldn't help it and went to Hollering and Laughing bout it too.

*T*HEY WAS A CROWD A'PEOPLE at the Jail House when me and Annie and Fritz got back over there, Papa said, and they was all pointing they Fingers at Poor o'Deputy Pahmeyer and a'Hollering at him bout who Murdered they Sheriff and the Judge and why hadn't he already gone off to catch em and the Deputy told em he had a Duty to Officiate at the Hanging of Calley Pearsall tomorra Noon and he'd go after em right after he done that but, Papa said, One Man hollered Well let's do the Hanging now then and be done with it and then all them others went to hollering Hang Him Hang Him Hang Him but Deputy Pahmeyer said No wouldn't be Right to do that when the Sentence is to Hang him Tomorra Noon and not Today and then the Man who was doing most a'the talking said You git out our way Elmer or we might Just Hang you in sted and hire us a'new Sheriff knows how the Cow eats the Corn round here. The Deputy was Scared to Death, Papa said, but drawed his self up and said You gonna have to wade through me Mister Fryberg fore you go to Hanging Mister Pearsall or any body else I know of but Oh then Mister Fryberg give the Deputy a Slap cross his Face knocked his Hat off and made his Eyes run water. I reckon you'll listen to me now won't you huh Deputy Pahmeyer, Mister Fryberg said, and Deputy Pahmeyer said Yes Sir Mister Fryberg I heared ever Word you said he said then Drawed Back and Slapped Mister Fryberg cross his Face hard as he could then took off a'Running down the Street and Mister Fryberg hollered Git Him Git Him and Oh, Papa said, the whole Bunch took off a'Running down the Street after o'Deputy Pahmeyer and then, he said, me and Annie give each other a Look cause now they wadn't no body a'Guarding the Jail House no more and we just stepped right on in Pretty as You Please and first thing we seen was the Jail Keys a'hanging there on the Wall like a Cookie to eat.

DON'T DO IT DON'T DO IT THEY'LL HANG YOU TOO, o'Calley said when I went to unlocking the Cell Door, Papa said, but No I done it any how cause I wadn't never gonna let no body Hang my o'Amigo Calley Pearsall if I could help it. Now they gonna wanna Hang you too he said and they ain't no Help for it. Oh and then his Eyes went to watering cause he was so scared for me and then I seen Annie was too same as Pela. Yall Ladies git on outta here, Calley said, I don't want yall having no part a'this. Me neither, Papa said, and give Annie a little push to go on out the Door with Pela but No she wadn't having none of it and give me a push back. You don't own me Mister, Annie said, I'll Hang right there long side you if I want to. But Calley give her and Pela both a Look and said you Ladies git on like I said. We can't be Breaking out a'Jail and be a'Worrying bout Yall both at the same time. You're Right and I hear ever word you say, Pela said then give him a Hug and a Kiss on his lips and said Come on Annie we don't want em getting caught cause a'us. Then, Papa said, Annie come over to me and give me a Hug and a Kiss too but it tasted like Salt cause her Tears was a'getting mixed up in it. You come back to me, she said, or I'm gonna come a'looking for you Don't matter where you go. I will Annie, I said, you don't have to Worry bout that. You better, she said, I ain't Fooling with you. Okay I said, Papa said, and Annie and Pela give each one a'us a'nother Hug and went on out. We got us a couple a'Good Ones there ain't we, Calley said, then went over there and got his big o'Pistola out the Drawer where they been a'Keeping it and put it back down his Pants where it come from in the First Place. I'm gonna get me one I said, Papa said, then took a pistol out the Drawer same as Calley done but he was already out the Door and didn't see me so I poked it down my Pants same as he done and went on out where he was a'saddling o'Firefoot and I went over there and unhitched Sister from Mister Pugh's Wagon then started putting my Momma's Mexkin Saddle on her quick's I could cause now here come Mister Fryberg and all them other Men back from where they caught o'Deputy Pahmeyer down the Street and Oh when they seen us a'Jumping on our Horses like that they drawed they guns and went to Shooting at us and Oh Listen Here we give em our Heels and hollered Yeehaa Yeehaa Yeehaa and lit a shuck on outta San Antoneya fast we could go with o'Fritz just a'barely keeping up back there behind us.

OH WE RUN AND WE RUN AND WE RUN, Papa said, and we didn't stop for nothing cep for o'Fritz to jump up on o'Sister with me. This is Bad Pookie o'Calley said when we finally stopped to let our Horses get em a'breath a'Air. Now they gonna be wanting to Hang You right there long side me, Calley said. I wouldn't have it no other way Mister Pearsall, Papa said, No Sir. Well you still just a Spud and don't know no Better is why, he said. Listen Some body go to putting a Noose round your neck and say it's all cause you been a'riding with Calley Pearsall Why you try to Look all innocent and say Calley Who Calley Who. No Sir I ain't gonna say that, Papa said, No Sir I ain't. Well it don't matter, Calley said, We both in the same Pickle now any how ain't we. Where we gonna go, Papa said. They ain't No Wheres we can go, Calley said. We Wanted Men now, he said. Wanted. You and Me both Mister and they gonna put it in the News-paper bout all the Banks we robbed and all the Cows we stole and how our Mommas is Crying bout how we turned out Bad when we was such good little Boys fore we went to Drinking and Chasing Womens. I ain't never been Drinking and Chasing Womens in my Life, Papa said. I didn't mean nothing by it, Calley said. You was just a'Joking me huh, Papa said, that's what I thought. Well I ain't Joking bout the Fix we in here Mister, he said, No Sir I ain't joking bout that. They gonna be People after us ever wheres you look. I might have to grow me a'Big Long Mustache just to keep em from knowing me. You reckon I could grow me one too, Papa said. No Sir You don't want one, Calley said, that'd just make it easier for em to Catch you. Well I don't know why, Papa said. Cause ever body in the County'd go to looking for that Boy got him a'Big Long Mustache and the first One to catch you gets the Reward. What Reward, Papa said. I don't know nothing bout no Reward. Gonna be One to catch me, o'Calley said, and a'nother One to catch you. How much is it, Papa said. I don't know, Calley said, I reckon its gonna be a'lot oncet we go to Robbing People and whatnot to make our Living. Course how much Reward probably gonna depend on if they want us Dead or a'Live ain't it, he said. Dead or a'Live, Papa said. Dead or a'Live. Yes Sir Dead or a'Live, Calley said. Them're Words make you set right up and pay attention ain't they.

COURSE HERE'S THE GOOD NEWS,

Calley said. Least they ain't gonna Hang me out there in front a'the Alamo Tomorra Noon are they. No Sir, Papa said, No Sir they ain't. While we talking bout it, Calley said, Lemme see that Pistol you took out the Drawer back in the Sheriff's Office when wadn't no body looking but me. So I handed him the Pistol from down my Pants and he took all the Bullets out and give it back. I don't want you Shooting no body, he said. Well how we gonna get they Money if they ain't scared a'us shooting em for it. If you wanna scare some body why don't you just show em you ugly Face, Calley said. You don't need no pistol. You Joking me again ain't you Mister Pearsall, Papa said. Yes I am, Calley said, and give me a'little Knock on my Head, Papa said, then went to twirling his Spur Ching e Ching e ChingChingChing and said I'm gonna miss Pela Rosa though ain't you gonna miss Annie. We ain't gonna be gone that long are we Mister Pearsall I said, Papa said, but o'Calley just looked way off out yonder some wheres and said That long and maybe a whole lot Longer you just can't never tell living the kind a'Life we gonna be a'Living. Course, he said, Ain't nobody even knows you was at the Jail when I took my Leave. You can go on back to San Antoneya right now and start you a good Life with your little Sweet Heart. No Sir I'm a'going with you, Papa said. Like Always. This ain't Like Always Mister, Calley said. I'm running for my Life now and you ain't. That don't make you no bettern me, Papa said, I don't see Why I can't go with you if I want to. Cause I don't want no Harm to come to you, Calley said, That's Why. That'd just break my Heart in two, he said. I can take care a'my self, Papa said, I won't be no Bother. No you never been no Bother in your Life, Calley said, and I never said that you was did I. No Sir you never did, Papa said, and I never said you did neither did I. No Sir not that I heared, Calley said then started scrunching his Bottom round in the Saddle. You getting ready to go ain't you Mister Pearsall, Papa said. Yes Sir I am, Calley said. No telling how manys already giving Chase from San Antoneya. Oh I was bout to Cry, Papa said. Will I ever see you again Mister Pearsall I said. I'm right there with you ever Day long as you got me in your Heart he said. Is that where you got me Mister Pearsall, Papa said. Oh Yes Sir it is he said then patted his Heart and give me one more little Knock on my Head to say Adios then give o'Firefoot his Heel and a'way they did go just a'kicking up big Clouds a'Dust like they wadn't nothing to it. And then, Papa said, they was gone and now it was just me and o'Fritz and Sister all a'lone out there in the Country by our self.

I DIDN'T KNOW WHAT TO DO,

Papa said. So I just set my self down on the Ground and tried to keep from Crying bout o'Calley being Gone and o'Fritz come over and set down there with me and in a minute we was both Crying but I give him a Scruff on his Head and said Fritz we gotta stop this or People gonna see us and think we just a couple a'o'Cry Babies a'missing our Momma and o'Fritz give me a Lick and said Heh Heh Heh bout it and then the o'Sun went down behind the Hill and the Moon come up and then of a sudden, Papa said, I looked over there and Why there was my o'Coyote Amigo Mister Pegleg a'Looking back at me and just a'Shimmering cause he already been Dead a'long time now. Oh Mister Pegleg I said, Papa said, I been a'Wondering if I was ever gonna see you again. And then he come over to me and give me a pull on my Pants Leg and I knowed he wanted to show me some thing so I follered him out in the Dark and in a minute I seen these two Men just Lost as they could be a'Shimmering round out there in the Cactus and both of em Crying bout it. Hey you Fellas I hollered, Papa said, and they looked over at me and Oh I knowed who they was right a'way. They was o'Dead Sheriff Highschoote and the Judge got murdered long with him. Who're you Sheriff Highschoote said. I'm the Fella stole your o'Mule, Papa said, but I thought it was some body else's Mule or I wouldn't a'stole it. What're yall doing out here any how. I don't have no Idea, the Judge said. I just took me one little Drink is all. No you had moren one, the Sheriff said, Let's not go to Storying bout it. Yall both Dead, Papa said. Don't yall know that. Dead, the Sheriff said. Dead, the Judge said. Yes Sir both a'yall just Deadern a'couple a'Clods out yonder in the Corn Field some where. Jesus H Lord Godamighty Christ, the o'Judge said. Dead. I wouldn't worry bout it, Papa said. I reckon some body'll come a'long here in a minute or two and take you to them Seven Old Men at they Table. What Seven Old Men you talking bout there Mister, the Sheriff said. Them Seven Old Men who see how all the Good Things you done in you Life stacks up a'gainst all the Bad Things you done and tell you if you got a'nother Life coming or you got to go on down there and set on a Flat Rock til Kingdom Come. Uh Oh the Sheriff said. Uh Oh the Judge said. I bet my Brother gonna come help me here in a minute Sheriff Highschoote said. He's the one went to poking o'Possum and Johnny and that poor Little o'One Eyed Bear with a Stick ain't he, Papa said, Ain't that your Brother. Well he might a'Poked him a Bear once or twice in his Life, the Sheriff said,

So What. Here's What, Papa said, your Brother probably already a'setting on his own Flat Rock down there for being mean to Creatures, so I don't believe I'd count on him helping you off Yours if you got one coming. Uh Oh Uh Oh, Sheriff Highschoote said. And here's a'nother thing, Papa said, You was gonna Hang o'Calley Pearsall for Murder when you knowed all a'long he just lost his Temper and hit your Brother too hard is all. They might think it was you a'trying to do a Murder on Mister Pearsall you self you know it. Uh Oh Uh Oh, Sheriff Highschoote said, Uh Oh Uh Oh.

*O*H THEN HERE COME THEM SEVEN OLD MEN, Papa said, and they set up they Table and Chairs under a Mesquite Tree then set down and give o'Sheriff Highschoote a'wave he oughta come set down there with em. I been a'setting all Day, the Sheriff said, I don't need to set no more. Sides that, he said, who the Hell Yall think Yall are to come over here and start a'Bossing me round like this any how. Don't matter Who we are, the Old Mexkin Man said, just only matters Who you are. Then he set a stack a'Black Dominoes and a stack a'White Dominoes down on the Table and said You get a White one for ever Good Thing you ever done in your Life and you get a Black One for ever Bad Thing you ever done. And then we see how they stack up against each other, the Old Chinaman said, and that's How we see Who you are down deep in your Heart. Well they was a'lot a'Things I might not a'wanted to do but I was the Sheriff and had to do em for the People, the Sheriff said. Me too, the Judge said, that's xactly how it was with me too Yes Sir. We didn't do nothing but What we had to do, Sheriff Highschoote said. Ask any body he said. Hell they voted for us didn't they. Did they, the Old Black Man said. That's some thing else we gonna have to talk bout here in a minute. Uh Oh the Judge said. Uh Oh the Sheriff said. Then the Old Mexkin Man looked over at me and said How come we always seeing you round here when it aint your Time yet. I don't know, Papa said, I reckon my o'Amigo Mister Pegleg just brings me here is all. The Old Mexkin Man reached down and give Mister Pegleg a Pet on his Head then, Papa said, and said I like this o'Fella here He's the bestest Singer I ever did hear in my Life then went to Yipping and a'Howling like a Coyote his self to show me what he was talking bout and then so did all them other Old Men

21

but Mister Pegleg put his Tail down tween his Legs and went on off in the Dark some wheres by his self to where he couldn't hear em. I don't think he liked it so much the Old Indian Man said. Well some Coyotes just get too big for they Britches if you ask me, the Old White Man said then looked over at me, Papa said, and said What you still doing here Mister. Well I got a question for these two Fellas here fore they go to stacking up they Black and White Dominoes if you Please, Papa said. Okay the Old Chinaman said then they all poked they Fingers in they Ears so they wouldn't know what I was asking. Who Murdered yall I said, Papa said. It was two Men, the Judge said, one of em had a Big Nose. And the other one, Sheriff Highschoote said, had Little Ears. But they was both mean SonsaBitches, the Judge said. Yes Sir they sure was the Sheriff said.

*N*EXT MORNING, Papa said, me and o'Fritz climbed up on Sister and went a'Riding through the Cactuses without no Breakfast but then here fore long we smelt some thing smelt like Bacon cooking on a Fire and heared a Bunch a'Men a'Laughing and a'Whooping bout it. I bet that's some Breakfast for us I said to Fritz, Papa said, then turned o'Sister to go see but No she didn't like it and wouldn't Go. Sister you been eating Grass all day and all night, Papa said, but me and o'Fritz here is bout to starve to Death and Blow a'way but she still didn't care and wouldn't Go. Okay then, Papa said, you stay here and we'll go see our self. So me and o'Fritz follered the Smell through the Woods but then of a sudden we seen through the Mesquites Trees bout ten twenty Men rolling this poor o'Black Man round and round in a big pile a'Chicken Feathers and Oh him just a'Hollering and a'Crying bout it but No they thought it was Funny and just kep a'Rolling him round like that and the Chicken Feathers a'Sticking to him til he looked like a Chicken his self and Oh it made me so Sad for that o'Black Man I pulled my pistol out my Pants and was gonna go over there and try to scare them Men a'way even if I didn't have no Bullets in my Gun. And I was just bout to do it, he said, when this Hand come down on my shoulder and this Whisper come in my Ear. Don't do it Sonny is what it said and I looked round, Papa said, and they was this Man a'squatting down there behind me. Just set tight, he said, they bout done with him now. Who are they any how to be so Mean to that o'Black Man, Papa said. They just a'bunch a Peckerwoods been Mean all they whole Life and don't know no better and that ain't no Black Man they Tarring and Feathering neither, the Man said. I'd go down there and help him my self cep they'd do the same god dam Thing to me. Then, Papa said, he pointed to one particular Man in the Bunch and said You see that Man there and I looked, Papa said, and I said Yes Sir I do see him. Well he's a Ring Tail Son of a Bitch the Man said and you don't never wanna mess with him in you Life you hear me. Yes Sir I do hear you I said, Papa said, but when I looked round the Man was a'sneaking a'way and now all them Others was too and in a minute they wadn't no body left cep that poor o'Man been Tarred and Rolled round in all them Chicken Feathers.

*M*E AND FRITZ WAITED A MINUTE, Papa said, then run over there and turned the Chicken Man over to see if he was still a'Live or Not and Yes he was so I pulled some Feathers off his Face and Oh then I seen who it was and who it was Was o'Deputy Pahmeyer. Then, he said, it come to me that Ring Tail Son of a Bitch the Man was a'talking bout was Mister Fryberg who Deputy Pahmeyer slapped in front a'the Jail House yesterday and this Tarring and Feathering was what he got back for it. I seen that Man done this to you, Papa said. He's the one you Slapped in the Face ain't he. May be I ought not a'done that, Deputy Pahmeyer said, cep he been Mean to me all his Life since we was just Little Chilren. Might a'been better to just gone on and Shot him, Papa said, might a'saved you all these Feathers here. Oh and then we went to plucking em off, Papa said, but they was just too many of em stuck in the Tar. We gonna have to give you a Bath in some Coal Oil to get em off, Papa said, that's all I know'll do it. I run by a Farm bout a'couple a'miles back, the Deputy said, I reckon they got some Coal Oil don't you. Well I hope so, Papa said, you don't wanna have to walk round looking like a Chicken all you Life do you.

${\mathcal B}$UT SISTER

wadn't bout to let no Chicken Man ride on her so poor o'Deputy Pahmeyer had to walk ever step and me and o'Fritz walked long with him to make him feel better bout it. They didn't Hang your Friend did they, he said, and I said No Sir he got a'way Papa said. How'd he do that the Deputy said. I reckon he had him some Help, Papa said. Good for you, the Deputy said. You being a good Friend to me now too ain't you. Yes Sir, Papa said. I always try to do Right when I can. Then that Afternoon, he said, we come to that Farm o'Deputy Pahmeyer was talking bout and I Helloed the House and this Woman come out a'hefting a big Gun. Where'd you catch that thing there she said and pointed her gun at my Chicken Man. This is Deputy Pahmeyer under all these Feathers, Papa said, you don't have to be a'scared a'him. Deputy Pahmeyer, she said, You the same Pahmeyer lived down yonder on Cotton Mouth Creek when you was just a Bare Foot Boy. Yes Ma'am that's me, the Deputy said. Do I know you. Well I reckon you did, she said. You didn't go and forget me did you. May be give him you name to help him remember Ma'am, Papa said. Leanda she said. Leanda Barnrock. Leanda Barnrock, Deputy Pahmeyer said, Leanda Barnrock. Yes Sir you remember me now don't you, she said. No Ma'am, Deputy Pahmeyer said, but it might just be my Feathers is a'itching me so Bad is why. You ain't neckid under all them Feathers are you Mister Pahmeyer, she said. Yes Ma'am I might be, he said. Well it don't matter, Leanda Barnrock said, Let's get the Coal Oil and give you a good warsh with it See if we can't find us a whole new Man under all that Mess.

${\mathcal S}$O MIZ BARNROCK

set her big Wash Tub out in the yard, Papa said, and Deputy Pahmeyer set down in it and Oh we both went to scrubbing on him with Coal Oil and Rags all but his Private Parts. No we tole him he was gonna have to scrub them Parts his self and he was glad to do it and Oh so many Chicken Feathers come a'floating up I believe you could a'made you a Feather Bed out em, Papa said. I'm sorry to be so much Trouble to you Leanda, Deputy Pahmeyer said. If I'd a'knowed it was you lived here I'd a'gone on to the next Farm to save you the Trouble. No that's okay Elmer, she said, I'm glad to

Where'd you catch that thing there she said
and pointed her gun at my Chicken Man.

see you again it's been so long. You never married huh. No Ma'am I never, Deputy Pahmeyer said. Just couldn't find no Woman good nough to suit you huh, she said. Well no Leanda I reckon it was more like I just couldn't find no Woman at all. Oh they traded a'Laugh bout that, Papa said, then she went to Work trying to scrub the Tar and Feathers out his Hair but they was just stuck too tight in the Tar. I got some Bad News for you Elmer she said. It can't be too Bad if it's a'coming from you Leanda, he said. I'm gonna have to cut all your Hair off if you wanna get shed a'these Feathers so you don't look like a Chicken no more. That's what that other Woman done to o'Samson that time ain't it, Deputy Pahmeyer said, And after that he was so weak from it he couldn't even bend over and ty his own shoes no more could he. That's cause she didn't feed him nothing after that, Miz Barnrock said, but I will you Elmer. Oh, Papa said, I didn't have no Idea what they was talkng bout but I seen they was some thing a'catching Fire there tween em. You ain't talking bout Maybe a Roasting Ear or some thing like that are you Leanda, Deputy Pahmeyer said. Too early for Roasting Ears, she said, but I can fix you some Pataters and Gravy if you think that'd do Elmer. Oh Yes Ma'am that'd do fine Leanda, he said, Papa said, then she said I'll go find my First Husband's o'Straight Razor and see if I can't shave the rest a'them Feathers off without a'cutting your head off like I done his. Oh and then me and o'Deputy Pahmeyer both give her a Look but she let go a'laugh, Papa said, and said Elmer if you'd a'Remembered me you'd a'Remembered I was always a'making a Joke but I ain't had much to Joke bout here lately til you come a'long a'wearing all your Feathers.

*A*FTER SHE SHAVED ALL HIS FEATHERS AND HAIR OFF, Papa said, Miz Barnrock give Mister Pahmeyer a Cook Pan to cover his Privates with then led him over to a'nother Wash Tub and give him a new Bath in Ly Soap and Water. I ain't never had moren one Bath in a Month he said but now look a'here I already had me two in one Day. You a Better Man for it Elmer, she said. Just lookee here and then, Papa said, she showed him what he looked like in this little hand Mirra she had and he just couldn't get over what he looked like now in his Shaved Head. I look like a Ball Peen Hammer a'walking round don't I he said. Yes Sir Elmer, Miz Barnrock said, you come here a Chicken Man and now you a Ball Peen Hammer Man ain't you and Oh, Papa said, they Laughed and Laughed bout it and then so did me and o'Fritz til we was all bout to fall down. I remember how Funny you was now when you was just a Girl Leanda, Deputy Pahmeyer said, I reckon I just forgot here in my Old Age. Oh, Papa said, seemed like ever thing they said back and forth was all Funny and I remember it was a Good Time.

That Evening after Miz Barnrock give Deputy Pahmeyer some a'her Dead Husbands old clothes, Papa said, me and the Deputy went down to the Barn and milked the Cow and Miz Barnrock come down there behind us in a minute and said That's a nice thing to do Mister Pahmeyer and Mister Pahmeyer said Well Leanda you been Nice to me all Day and I just wanted to be Nice to you back is all. Well if you want to, she said, you can stay here and be Nice to me all you want to I wouldn't mind it. Well I preciate that Deputy Pahmeyer said but I got some thing I got to do back in San Antoneya. He's Deputy Sheriff there you know Miz Barnrock I said, Papa said, that's Why ain't it Deputy Pahmeyer. No Sir they's some thing else I got to do. What's that Elmer, Miz Barnrock said, if you don't mind me asking. Well, Deputy Pahmeyer said, you remember that Boy in our School used to chunk Rocks and knock all them little Baby Birds out they Nest so the Cats could eat em. O'Ken Fryberg that's who you talking bout there ain't it Elmer she said. He was always a Mean Boy his whole Life wadn't he. Yes Ma'am o'Ken Fryberg, the Deputy said, he's the one sicced all them others on me with they Tar and Feathers. And that ain't all neither he said. What else Elmer, Miz Barnrock said. Well I ain't just gonna walk off and let it go this time is What Else Leanda, he said.

*T*HAT NIGHT AFTER SUPPERS when Miz Barnrock took the Scraps out to the Cats, Papa said, I seen her reach down and pick up some a'Deputy Pahmeyers o'Tarred Hair from where she threw it after she cut it off his Head and stick it in her Pocket. I didn't have no Idea why she done such a thing but I was already old nough to know Womens do things don't make no Sense all the time any how. Then when she come back in the House and Deputy Pahmeyer said Leanda I feel kind a'Funny a'wearing your Husbands old clothes like this and she said Don't worry bout it Elmer he's already Dead as he's ever gonna be and don't need em no more. What took him, Deputy Pahmeyer said. A Snake didn't jump up and bite him did it. A Snake, she said, Oh Lord No he was a Snake his self then laughed when she seen the Look on our Face and said Naw I just said that cause I'm always saying Funny Things so I don't lose my mine a'living out here all by my self on this o'Hard Scrabble piece a'Dirt. Why Leanda, Deputy Pahmeyer said, you'd never know it was any thing but Peaches and Cream out here the way you look so Pretty. You always doing Nice Things for me Elmer, she said, and now you a'saying Nice Things too. No I mean it ever Word I say he said. I seen a'lot a ugly Womens in my Life but you ain't one of em Leanda. Oh she Looked over at me then, Papa said, and said See what I mean bout him. He don't have to do no moren open his Mouth and out comes a'Bucket a'Honey don't it. Yes Ma'am it does I said then me and o'Fritz went on out to the Barn and give Sister some Hay to eat and a good Petting. And then in a minute, Papa said, here come o'Deputy Pahmeyer to make his Bed. You and Miz Barnrock getting to be pretty good Friends by the Look a'it ain't you Deputy Pahmeyer I said. Yes Sir we are, he said, I almost wish I didn't have that Busness I got to tend to back in San Antoneya. Well you gonna come right on back here after that ain't you, Papa said. Well I might not even be able to come back Deputy Pahmeyer said, but wouldn't say no more bout it and went on to Bed.

*S*OME THING BOUT IT BOTHERED ME so bad I couldn't sleep, Papa said, so after o'Deputy Pahmeyer went to Snorting and Snoring I sneaked out the Barn and went on back up to the House to tell Miz Barnrock bout it but fore I knocked on the door I seen her through the Winder a'washing the Tar out a'them pieces a Deputy Pahmeyers Hair she had hid in her pocket and then, he said Why she stuck em up under her nose like a little Mustache with a piece a'Tar. Oh and then, he said, she grabbed her little Hand Mirra and went to trimming on it til she was Happy bout how it Looked on her and course, Papa said, I thought she just gone total Loonie and went on back to the Barn and didn't say nothing bout how I was thinking the reason o'Deputy Pahmeyer was a'going back to San Antoneya was to Shoot that man Fryberg for making Fun a'him all his Life

28

and getting all them others to Tar and Feather him like he done here just today. So I tickled Deputy Pahmeyer on his Ear with a Feather and he went to swatting at it and waked up and give me a Bad Look. Don't never do that a'gain he said, I had bout all the Feathers I want for a good long while now. I need to talk to you I said, Papa said. Well I'm a'wake now he said, what's a'Holding you back. You ever hear a'the Devil's Fork Deputy Pahmeyer, Papa said. It's what the o'Devil sticks you with when he's trying to drive you to the Fire but you won't go he said. No Sir, Papa said, it's a Direction in the Road and if you take the Wrong One you maybe ain't never gonna be able to get back on the Right One again in your Life. Why you telling me all this Mister, o'Deputy Pahmeyer said, I'm trying to sleep. Well, Papa said, I just wouldn't want you a'taking the Devil's Fork when you go back in San An- toneya Tomorra is all. Deputy Pahmeyer give it a good long Thought, Papa said, then just shook his o'Ball Peen Head like it was the Saddest thing in the World and said No Sir Leanda just wouldn't never have a Man people was always going round making Fun of.

*B*RIGHT AND EARLY NEXT MORNING, Papa said, they was a knock on the Barn Door and when we opened it why there was Miz Barnrock all Dressed to go some wheres in her Wagon. Elmer, she said, I got a Favor I need to ask you. Course Leanda, Deputy Pahmeyer said, just ask it. I got to take some things over to my Sister and I need you to watch the Place so don't nobody walk off with it while I'm gone. Course Leanda he said. Only just take me a Day or two she said, I don't think no moren that. Course Leanda he said. You a nice Man Elmer she said. Well you a nice Woman Leanda he said. I reckon we just two Peas in a Pod ain't we Elmer, she said. I reckon so, he said. Well ain't we Elmer she said and I could see she wanted to make sure of it, Papa said. Yes Ma'am we are, Elmer said. We sure are. Okay I'll be back Maybe even bring you a Surprise she said and went on off, Papa said, and I seen she had some more a'her Dead Hus- band's Clothes in the back a'her Wagon and his Hat too. Well I reckon this is where we get to see if we was meant to be Farmers or not then huh, Deputy Pahmeyer said. I already been one, Papa said, and don't wanna be a'nother one neither. I think I might like it, Deputy Pahmeyer said, I don't believe

I'd mine wiggling my Toes in the Dirt all day long behind some o'Mule pulling a plow and some good Woman a'bringing me cool Water to drink when I'm thirsty. I ain't never heared a'no Farm like that in my Life, Papa said. I think you just a'Dreaming ain't you Deputy Pahmeyer. I don't know, he said, I might be I might be. You ain't gonna be no Farmer and not nothing else neither you go to taking the Devil's Fork Deputy Pahmeyer, Papa said. You might wanna run that round in your Head a'little fore its too Late, Papa said. Thank you, he said, But I can't be no Farmer til I'm a Man first.

*T*HEN COUPLE A'DAYS LATER, Papa said, here come Miz Barnrock back from her Sister's Place and she was all Bright and Sunny bout it. I missed you Elmer, she said. Did you Miss me too. Well Yes I did miss you Leanda, he said, but they's some other things in front a'my mine and it was Hard to get pass em. You talking bout that Busness you still got back in San Antoneya ain't you Elmer she said, Papa said. Yes I am, Deputy Pahmeyer said. I been trying but it just won't go a'way from me. I want him to try some more, Papa said. I been a'telling him that but he won't listen to me. Well you only got to look at him a'minute to know how Hard Headed he is Miz Barnrock said then reached over and pulled the Deputy's o'Ear to let him know she was just only Joking him. My first Husband wadn't so much Hard Headed as he was just plain Stupid she said. How else you reckon you own Mule gonna plow over you in the Corn Field. That's a Sad Story ain't it Miz Barnrock, Papa said. Yes Sir she said but I've heared worser ones from up in Gillespee County where I lost a Second Cousin to a Wast Sting or may be he was a First Cousin. Yes I think may be he was, Miz Barnrock said, and it was that One Legged Boy over yonder in Hayes County was the Second. I got to go if I'm a'going, Deputy Pahmeyer said, even if that is a Intresting Story you a'telling there Leanda. I wish you wouldn't, Papa said. You already said that bout a hunderd times Mister, Deputy Pahmeyer said, now just leave it go cause I'm a'going any how. But you a'coming back ain't you Elmer, Miz Barnrock said. That's all I need to know so I can Sleep at night. I can't say Yes Leanda, Deputy Pahmeyer said, but I can't say No neither. Well you ain't lost your Tongue have you Elmer, she said. What can you say. Well, he said, I reckon all I can say is I'll Come Back if I am able to

30

Come Back. You mean that Elmer she said, Papa said, and then he said Yes I do mean that Leanda. Okay she said Go on and Do what you got to Do you just a'wasting Ever Body's Time a'talking bout it here.

*C*OUPLE A'DAYS LATER, Papa said, Why here come o'Deputy Pahmeyer back from San Antoneya and he looked ever bit Bright and Sunny bout it as Miz Barnrock did when she come a'riding back from her Sister's Place the other Day. Elmer, she said, I am Glad to see you Sir then, Papa said, she give him a big Smile and he give it right back to her and said I bout run all the way back Leanda. That mean somebody's a'Chasing you, Papa said. No Sir, Deputy Pahmeyer said, ain't no body a'Chasing me No Sir not a'one. What bout that Busness you was talking bout you had to do with that Man, Papa said. Well, Deputy Pahmeyer said, some body else come a'long and done that Busness with o'Fryberg fore I even got there to do mine so I just drinked me a Beer in the Buckhorn to Celebrate and come on back. Who was it done the Busness, Papa said. No Sir don't nobody know, Deputy Pahmeyer said. This Man just come up behind o'Fryberg a'standing there at the Bar and said I think I know you don't I Mister. You bout the sorriest Son of a Bitch they ever was in the World ain't you and then o'Fryberg turned round and said If you knowed me you'd know I'm bout to Whup your Rusty o'Butt for a'Bothering me like this when I'm a'having my Refreshment here. Oh and then, Deputy Pahmeyer said, when o'Fryberg drawed back to hit the Man with his Fist why the Man let go with a'Big Gun he had hid up under his coat and blowed o'Fryberg all the way up in the Rafters. And then, he said, the Man walked out the Door like he never even been there in the First Place. And you saying no body even knowed the Man huh, Miz Barnrock said. No no body never even seen him be fore, Deputy Pahmeyer said. They say he probably wadn't from round there no wheres. I seen Miz Barnrock give a little Smile to her self then, Papa said, and I said Well I'm glad it wadn't no Woman done it. Deputy Pahmeyer laughed and said Well if it was a Woman she growed her a'Mustache cause they say this Fella done the Shooting had him a little scraggly one up under his Nose looked like some thing come off a'Skunk Tail.

OH AND HERE'S SOME THING ELSE,
Deputy Pahmeyer said then come out his Pocket with a Hand Bill that said
WANTED CALLEY PEARSALL FOR MURDER AND JAIL BREAK. AND
WITH HIM THE BOY SIN NOMBRE. REWARD. REWARD. REWARD. I admit, Papa said, it irritated me some o'Calley taken up with some other Boy
and not me. Who's that Boy they talking bout there I said. Ain't no body
knows Deputy Pahmeyer said. Sin Nombre means No Name. Could be any
body he said. Could even be You I reckon huh. Then he give me a little Wink
bout it and said You the one opened the Jail Door for him wadn't you. He's
the Best Friend I ever did have in my Life, Papa said, so don't go eating on
me bout it Mister. No I ain't, the o'Deputy said. I might a'done it my self if
I'd a'had a little more Spunk. Well you can be Spunky right here from now
on Elmer, Miz Barnrock said. You ain't got no more Busness back in San
Antoneya the Rest a'your Life do you. No Ma'am I don't that I know of. Who
put this Hand Bill out any how, Papa said. I thought o'Sheriff Highschoote
was Dead. O'Mayor Ludwig a'pointed him a new Sheriff and here's the Surprise You already know him. Simon Pugh, he said, you remember him and
his Little Brother Johnny don't you. You ain't really telling me Mister Pugh
is the new Sheriff are you, Papa said. Yes Sir and ever body says he sure can
Crack the Whip when he wants to and most ever body in San Antoneya is already going round a'Scared of him. Him and the Mayor must a'been Friends
back there some wheres to get that Job so Quick huh, Miz Barnrock said.
No Leanda, I think Mister Pugh just give him some Money for it, Deputy
Pahmeyer said. Like always. But this is Good News for Mister Pearsall aint
it, Papa said. Mister Pugh ain't never gonna let no body Hang him cause
a'what o'Calley done for his Little Brother. He ain't Singing that Tune now
Mister, the Deputy said. What I heared was o'Calley Pearsall and this Sin
Nombre Fella here is the First Ones he's a'going after cause he knows what
they look like and when he catches em he says he's gonna Hang em Two at a
Time. Oh Boy Hidy, Papa said, I didn't know what to think bout all this. La
Vida Brinca I said, Papa said, and Miz Barnrock said that's Mexkin for some
thing or other ain't it and I said Yes Ma'am means Life Jumps. Yes Sir it sure
does don't it she said then give o'Deputy Pahmeyer a'little Pet on his o'Ball
Peen Head like she owned him now.

. . . the Man let go with a'Big Gun he had hid
up under his coat and blowed o'Fryberg all
the way up in the Rafters.

I RECKON I BETTER GO FIND MISTER PEARSALL and tell him, Papa said. I reckon he already knows, Deputy Pahmeyer said, He can read can't he. Read and Write both I reckon huh. Oh Yes Sir, Papa said, Knows bout ever thing they is to Know. I didn't get to Know him much but I liked what I did Know bout him, Deputy Pahmeyer said. He can hide in the Barn if he wants to, Miz Barnrock said, You can too. No Ma'am I got to go on and Go, Papa said. I'm already worried bout Sick for him. Well yall got a Hide Out here any time you want it she said. Just gonna be me and Mister Pahmeyer a'Living here ain't that right Elmer and Deputy Pahmeyer said Yes it is and I Thank You Leanda.

Then Me and Sister and o'Fritz rode on out, Papa said, but not having no good Idea where to but then I got to thinking I bet o'Calley went up the Country to Gonzales County where his Sister Eurica lives cause he always been a'saying that was one more Fish he still got to Fry ever since the o'Sheriff a'Comal County shot and killed her Husband Jack Ivy the Third and sides that I didn't have no better Idea where to look any how. So we just went a'riding on up the Country in the genral Direction a'Gonzales County best I could tell, Papa said, and it wadn't long and me and o'Fritz both couldn't help it and went on off to sleep there on my Momma's Mexkin Saddle as we was riding a'long and, he said, it just couldn't a'been no nicer but then of a sudden some body said Hold your Horses there a minute Mister and I opened my Eye and Oh they was two Men a'standing there in the road with they Hats pushed back on they Head and they Teeth just a'shining even if they didn't have all that many to Shine but one of em had a Big Nose and the other one had Little Ears. Where you a'going Mister, Big Nose said, and I said Up to Gonzales County to tell my o'Amigo Calley Pearsall the new Sheriff a'San Antoneya is a'Looking for him. You ain't talking bout o'Simon Pugh are you, Little Ears said. Yall know him I said, Papa said. Oh they went to Laughing bout it and o'Big Nose said Know him Why Hell Mister we been a'Robbing Banks and Such with him most all our Life. Yes Sir that's right, Little Ears said, up to when that tricky Son of a Bitch run off with all our Money.

find this Calley Pearsall Fella you a'looking for, o'Big Nose said, How bout that. Course we'd give you a'little Taste a'the Reward Money, Little Ears said, we ain't stingy with our Money. Or here's a'nother Idea, Big Nose said, we might just go on and turn you in for the Reward Money what you think bout that Sin Nombre. No, Little Ears said, we gonna need him for Bait to catch that other one first. Yall ain't never gonna catch o'Calley Pearsall in your Life, Papa said. He's too smart and his Horse is way too Fast for Yall. Maybe so but I don't reckon he'd ever just run off and leave you in a Pickle would he, Big Nose said. I ain't in no Pickle I said, Papa said, But Little Ears pulled out his Pistol and said Oh Yes you are Senyor Sin Nombre. Now get a'going fore I throw your little Piss Ant of a Dog there out the Winder and o'Fritz grinned at him for it then went Heh Heh Heh but, Papa said, he wadn't trying to be Funny bout it. Where is Gonzales County any how, Big Nose said and I said I don't have no Idea Mister. Well where we a'going then Little Ears said and I said I don't know We just a'going and I reckon we'll get some wheres or other here fore long and when we do we can ask some body there where we at. Then I said, Papa said, Yall the ones tied o'Mister Pugh to that Tree and then run off and Left him Neckid ain't you. We was just trying to get our Share a'the Money but he wouldn't tell us where it was Big Nose said. They was a False Bottom in his Wagon and he had it hid in there under a'Pile a'Sand, Papa said. Oh they both went to Laughing bout that, Papa said, and o'Big Nose said Why that wiley o'Son of a Bitch he always got a Trick or two in his Bag don't he. Don't he, Little Ears said. You just got to hand it to him I reckon. Why don't yall just go after Mister Pugh sted a'Mister Pearsall, Papa said. You know right where he is and it ain't that Far over to San Antoneya from here as it is from here to Gonzales County how ever Far that is. No Sir we like having a Sheriff for a Friend, Little Ears said. Yes Sir but what yall gonna do when he Hangs you for Murdering Sheriff Highschoote and that Judge. We didn't Murder no Sheriff and some Judge did we, Little Ears said. Not that I know of less you talking bout them two Men was Dancing round Drunk as a Goat in front a'they Camp Fire the other Night, Big Nose said. That's them, Papa said. Oh, Little Ears said, Well then we did. And that o'Farm Boy we come up on too, Big Nose said. Don't forget bout him.

WHY CAN'T WE JUST BE FRIENDS,

Papa said, since we all already Out Laws together any how ain't we and Mister Pearsall one too. A Out Law don't have no Friends, Little Ears said. Just maybe one or two his whole Life. You take o'Simon Pugh, Big Nose said, we thought he was a Friend a'ours but No he stole our share a'the Money one day and that ain't no Friend is it. No Sir I don't reckon so, Papa said. So now, Little Ears said, all we got is each other for a Friend ain't that Right Mathias. Yes Sir just each other for a Friend Big Nose said. We might could let you be a Friend after you been the Bait. No Sir, Papa said, I don't wanna be your Friend and I ain't never gonna be the Bait if you talking bout using me to catch Calley Pearsall. You gonna have to find you some other Bait some wheres else. You gonna be a'Singing a different Tune here fore we done with You, Little Ears said, ain't he Mathias. Ain't he, Big Nose said, Yes sir ain't he. No I ain't, Papa said. That's the only Tune I got to sing. Well you know what they say bout Bait, o'Big Nose said. No whatta they say bout Bait Mathias, Little Ears said. They say it don't matter it's Live Bait or Dead Bait it's still Bait, Big Nose said. But I didn't say nothing back, Papa said, and we just kep a'riding on to Gonzales County even if we didn't have no good Idea where it was. This gonna be a long Trip ain't it Albert o'Big Nose said and Little Ears said Yes Sir Long Long Long Trip less we can find us some body to Rob on the way and get us some Money to Live on.

THAT THING O'CALLEY TOLE ME

bout what ever you a'Looking for in this World is a'Looking for you too, Papa said, was True just the same for these two here as for any body else and so wadn't long and we come cross this Old Man and his Old Wife a'hauling a'Load a'Cotton some wheres or other to the Market. I bet they carrying some Money on em don't you Little Ears said and o'Big Nose said Yes I reckon they are too Whatta you think Sin Nombre. I don't care they are or not, Papa said, I ain't gonna Rob no body. Well why wouldn't you, Little Ears said, you already on the Wanted List ain't you. I ain't on there for Robbery, Papa said, I'm on there for Jail Break. They put you in the Jail House for either one of em, Big Nose said, or Hang you One. Hell they don't care a'Lick which. I don't wanna start Robbing People, Papa said, that ain't the Fork I wanna take. Well we can't just leave you here Little Ears said, how bout we just ride down there and ask em where Gonzales County is and go on. But not Rob em huh, Papa said. Oh Hell No not Rob them Poor Old People he said, just ask em a question bout where is Gonzales County at is all. Well I wouldn't mine that I don't reckon, Papa said. Well we got us a Bargain here then don't we, o'Big Nose said and we rode on down the Hill and give them Old People a sign to Stop they wagon and when they did why Little Ears pointed his Finger at me, Papa said, and said Yall know who this Fella here is and the Old Woman said Yes that's o'Man Smiley's Boy Nimrod ain't it. No it ain't neither the Old Man said. Well Who is it then you know so much his o'Wife said and he said I didn't say I knowed Who it was I just said it wadn't Who you said it was. Well if I tell you Who it is Little Ears said, I want your promise you won't go telling no body else okay. Okay the Old Man said, and so did the Old Woman, Papa said. Its Sin Nombre the Boy Out Law is Who it is, Little Ears said. How you like that. Who the Old Woman said. Who the Old Man said and then I said, Papa said, That's just a Name they give me but I ain't no Boy Out Law. Any chance yall know what Direction Gonzales County is. Not me the Old Woman said. Not me neither the Old Man said. Then, Papa said, o'Big Nose drawed his Pistol out his Pants and said Okay we gonna have to take all you Money then.

AND THEN WHEN WE WAS A'RIDING OFF, Papa said, Little Ears ask Big Nose How much Money'd we get off them two Old People and Big Nose said Bout a Dollar. That's probably all the Money they got in the World, Papa said, Yall bout the Meanest Robbers I ever seen in my Life. No we a'lot Meanern that ain't we Mathias, Little Ears said. Yes I'd say we are Big Nose said. Why'd yall go and tell them Old People I was a Boy Out Law any how, Papa said, when I ain't no such a Thing. Let's tell him Why, Big Nose said and Little Ears said The more People think you Sin Nombre the Boy Out Law the more better it is for us is Why. Cause the Reward Money gonna get Bigger and Bigger he said and then when it gets Big nough why we gonna turn you in for it and go Whoop it up some wheres else on what they pay us. I ain't gonna Rob no body, Papa said. I wouldn't feel Right bout it. Don't matter you feel Right bout it or Not, Big Nose said,

People still gonna think you a Robber cause you gonna be right there with us when we go to Robbing. Oh I seen I was trapped, Papa said, and couldn't see no way out a'it. Yall better be Careful I don't turn yall in for the Reward in sted, Papa said. How much you reckon you'd get for o'Albert here, Big Nose said. I don't know but I bet it's a'Bunch cause Yall was the ones Murdered o'Sheriff Highschoote and the Judge and that other Fella you was talking bout. Here's a Idear, Big Nose said, Say we turn o'Albert in and get the Reward Money for him then turn right round and Break him back out a'the Jail again and then, he said, if you wanted to you could turn me in for some more Reward Money then break me right back out a'gain like we done Him after you get it. Don't that sound good, o'Big Nose said. You wouldn't just leave me there would you, Little Ears said, and then run off with that first Reward Money would you. No I never even thought a'that Albert, Big Nose said, but that's a Funny Idear ain't it. Wouldn't be Funny to me if I was the One left a'setting there in the Jail House, Little Ears said. I'm just talking Albert, Big Nose said, I wouldn't never do that. Well you just said you thought it'd be Funny if you was to, Little Ears said. Yes Sir but I ain't never gonna, Big Nose said. I don't like it and I ain't a'gonna do it, Little Ears said. My answer is No bout it. My answer is No too, Big Nose said. It just come to me you might Leave me in the Jail House when it's your Turn to get the Reward Money. Oh, Papa said, I didn't know how long they been Friends in they Life but they wadn't One now.

*B*IG NOSE AND LITTLE EARS tied me to a'Ellum Tree that Night so I wouldn't run off on em, Papa said, and o'Fritz went to bed in my Lap like wadn't nothing going on. Why don't you bite this Rope in two, I said, and let's you and me and o'Sister go a'Tip Toeing on down the Road but No o'Fritz was sound a'Sleep even when some o'Owl went a'Hoot Hoot Hooting some wheres and wouldn't Quit it til Big Nose or Little Ears one or the other hollered Pipe Down you o'Son of a Bitch. You ain't talking to me are you Albert, Big Nose said. No I ain't talking to you Mathias, Little Ears said. Cause a'what you said bout putting me in the Jail House and getting the Reward for it I thought maybe you was still Mad I wouldn't do it and was a'calling me a Son of a Bitch for it, Big

Nose said. Go to Sleep, Little Ears said. You a'bothering me now. No you the one a'bothering me, Big Nose said. You go to Sleep then I will too. Well I can't go to Sleep long as you a'Jabbering like this, Little Ears said. I'm bout to come over there and Whomp you with a Stick or some thing you don't shut up and be quiet he said. I couldn't see em in the Dark, Papa said, but I could hear em and Oh I could tell they was bout to lose they Temper at one a'nother. You try to hit me with a Stick or some thing, Big Nose said, I'll shoot you Deadern a god dam Fence Post and you know I will too don't you. I ain't a'scared a'you Mathias if that's what you been a'thinking, Little Ears said. Well maybe it's bout time you get a'scared a'me, Big Nose said, cause I'm bout to come over there and Stomp on you like I would a'Bug. No you ain't, Little Ears said. Yes I am, Big Nose said. Yes Sir I sure as Hell am. Well here I am, Little Ears said, come on then you Son of a Bitch. By god I might, Big Nose said. You better be careful you Son of a Bitch. Oh and then I heared One or the Other cock his Pistol back then I heared the Other One cock his back too. Yall better stop I said, Papa said, Yall gonna be a'Shooting at each other here in a minute and somebody's gonna get Hurt. Hell o'Mathias couldn't hit the Shit House Door if he was in there a'setting on the Hole, Little Ears said. Oh and then o'Big Nose said that's all the Guff I'm a'taking off you Mister and let go a BOOM, Papa said, then Little Ears let go a couple his self BOOM BOOM and Oh then they Pistols just went to flashing like Lightning in a'Storm BOOM BOOM BOOM BOOM BOOM.

OH THEN IT GOT JUST QUIET AS SOME LITTLE O'MOUSE, Papa said, and me and o'Fritz just set there waiting for what ever was coming next and what come next was one of em a'saying Help Me Help Me Help Me and I said, Papa said, which one a'yall is a'saying that and o'Big Nose said it's me Mathias Henly. Help Me Help Me Help Me, he said. I can't Help you, Papa said, Yall got me tyed to this Tree over here. Did you just kill your Friend. Well I don't hear him Talking do you he said. No Sir but you don't reckon he's just a'Playing Possum on you do you I said, Papa said, then they was a'nother BOOM and Big Nose said Well he ain't a'Playing Possum no more now if he was then. You gonna Help me or not. I would, Papa said, but I already said yall got me tyed to this Tree and I can't do nothing but

Squirrel round on my Bottom a'little. Well maybe I can crawl over there and unty you and you can Help me then, Big Nose said, how bout that Senyor Nombre. Yes Sir come on if you can, Papa said. I ain't a'going no wheres. That little Dog a'yours ain't gonna bite me is he, he said. I'll tell him not to, Papa said, you don't have to worry bout him. I had me a Little Dog when I was in the War did you know that, Big Nose said. No Sir, Papa said, I didn't even know you was in the War. Oh Yes Sir I was, he said, Hottest god dam Time I ever did see in my Life. Are you gonna crawl over here or you just wanna tell Stories, Papa said. Where are you any how, o'Big Nose said, I can't hardly see in all this Dark and it's getting Darker and Darker all the Time ain't it. Just try to come to my Voice, Papa said, Reckon you can do that. What, he said, I can't but hardly hear you Mister Nombre. Just come Here to me, Papa said. HERE HERE HERE HERE HERE Can you Hear me now. I knowed he was a Goner, Papa said, and it wadn't no use but I kep a'talking any how. What ever happened to your Little Dog I said. What's that you a'saying Mister, o'Big Nose said. I said that Little Dog you had in the War with you, Papa said, what ever happened to him. Oh him, Big Nose said. Yes Sir, Papa said, you take him Home with you after the War is that what you done. No course not, Big Nose said, we had to eat him long fore that. Me and o'Albert. Where is o'Albert, he said. He's over there some wheres, Papa said, I can't see in the Dark neither. Albert where you at, Big Nose said. Albert Albert Albert. I think he's already Dead, Papa said. Dead, o'Big Nose said. Dead. Albert's Dead. I didn't even know he was sick. Oh No Albert's Dead, he said, Oh No Oh No Oh No Oh No and just kep a'saying it, Papa said, til he couldn't say it no more and not nothing else in the World neither.

THEN ME AND O'FRITZ

just had to set there like that the rest a'the Night, Papa said, but just fore the Sun come up o'Fritz went to Low Growling bout some thing or other and then the Sun did come up and Oh I seen he was a'Growling at a Family a'Havalina Hogs that was over there a'eating on them Two's Fingers and Toes. Git you Hogs I said, Papa said, Git Git Git but No they was Happy where they was and wouldn't go. Then he said o'Fritz made a Run and a Jump at em but Big Bore Hog bout Tusked him and he run on back over to

. . . and Oh I seen he was a'Growling at a Family a'Havalina Hogs that was over there a'eating on them Two's Fingers and Toes.

me quick's he could. Fritz you gonna get you self kilt that way if you ain't careful I said and then Oh here come some Buzzerds from down out the Sky and they went to eating on them two Dead Men too and then a Fox and some Coyotes the same thing. Oh all day long they was just a'eating a'way on them Two but ever oncet in a'while they'd look over at me there a'tyed to that Ellum Tree and Lick they Lips cause they knowed I was gonna be they Dessert. Oh and then I seen a'Line a'Ants coming back from there a'Carrying little pieces a'them two Fellas in they Pinchers, Papa said, and I said to my self they ain't gonna be nothing left a'them o'Robbers here in a'minute. Just they Bones is all and then them Ants gonna come over here and start to Eating on me too ain't they and Oh I said to my self Yes Sir that is xactly what they gonna do and then, Papa said, why that Big o'Bore Hog give me a look and smacked his Lips and clacked his o'Teeth Clack Clack Clack like that and then Oh here he come, he said, and I started a'looking round ever wheres to see if they was Any Body or Any Thing could save me but No wadn't No Thing or No Body no wheres at all to save me. Oh, Papa said, Oh Oh Oh.

*B*UT OF A SUDDEN, Papa said, some body threw a Rock and hit that big o'Bore Hog on his Nose and he run off and went back to eating on one a'them others and next thing they was this Voice come up behind me said Why you in a Pickle here ain't you Senyor Sin Nombre but I said No Sir I ain't cause I knowed that voice was my o'Amigo Calley Pearsall a'doing the Talking and not no other. And Oh Boy Hidy I was glad of it too, he said. I been a'looking for you Mister Pearsall, Papa said. I reckon you been a'looking for me too huh. Well I'm a'headed over to Gonzales, Calley said, to Fry them other Fish I been a'telling you I got to Fry and come this way cause right over yonder is where Plum Creek runs in with the San Marcos River and Right there is where I always wanna get me a Drink a'water cause that's where the wild Plums fall in and make the water Sweet. You mean you wadn't looking for me I said, Papa said, and o'Calley said Well I reckon they was some part a'me a'looking for you or I wouldn't a'never come here to this particular Spot when you was in your Pickle. Things just get in the Air some times is all, he said, and I learned if you don't think bout em too much Why they'll blow you to where you oughta been a'going in the First Place.

Your Sister Eurica is them other Fish you still got to Fry ain't she, Papa said. Yes Sir I still ain't tole her Her Husband Jack Ivy the Third is Dead and Gone, he said. I reckon I just been putting it off cause she's bout the Worsted Person they ever Was or ever gonna Be. These two Fellas here was Bad too, Papa said, they used to make they Living robbing People with o'Simon Pugh the new Sheriff a'San Antoneya did you know that Mister Pearsall. No Sir but it don't surprise me, o'Calley said. Most a'the Law Men I knowed in my Life was always a'Jumping the Fence back and forth tween Good and Bad they self. Well these two here ain't never gonna Jump no Fence ever a'gain in they Life are they, Papa said. No Sir not on they own two Feets any how by the Look a'it, Calley said. Some body come a'long and Shoot em or what, he said. No Sir they got Mad at each other and done it to they self, Papa said. Well see, o'Calley said, Didn't I tell you one time Bad Things is what comes a'losing your Temper if you ain't careful. Well I reckon you the one to know bout that, Papa said. Wadn't it you a'losing your Temper at that Man a'poking o'Possum and Johnny and that poor Little o'One Eyed Bear that got you in all this Mess you in here. Yes Sir, o'Calley said. That is xactly what I'm a'talking bout.

*M*E AND O'CALLEY tyed them two Dead Robbers on they Horse and turned em a'loose for some body else to find, Papa said, and Calley said No telling what them Two gonna be telling People bout how they come to this Bad End. Well they both Dead ain't they, Papa said, I don't reckon they gonna be Telling no body much a'nothing. Oh you gonna be surprised what People gonna hear from em don't matter a Lick if these two o'Boys here is Dead or not. Course First Thing People gonna think is o'Sin Nombre is the one Murdered em in they Sleep when they wadn't looking. Oh I never, Papa said, No Sir I never. And here's a'nother thing Senyor Nombre, Calley said, you got to quit Robbing Old People. Why I never Robbed no Old People in my Life and not no body else neither, Papa said, who said that bout me. Why them Old People you Robbed said it, Calley said. They come on in to Town and said you Robbed em then you and your Little Dog rode off just a'Laughing bout it and a'counting the Money. No Sir I never I never, Papa said, I never. Here's some more Bad news Senyor Nombre, Calley said, them two Old People gonna place you with these two Dead Men a'riding off here now and ever body gonna say Oh that Boy Sin Nombre ain't only just a Robber but he's a Murderer to Boot ain't he. They ain't gonna say that bout me, Papa said. Are they. You just watch and see, Calley said. Yes Sir and I'm sorry bout it too, he said. Oh I was Sick bout it, Papa said, and Urped up on the Ground in front a'me and o'Calley give me a Pet on my Back while I was a'doing it and said Try not to Urp too much they ain't nothing'll wear a Man out quickern Urping less it's some Woman you know it. What am I gonna do bout this Mister Pearsall, Papa said. Ever body's gonna wanna Hang me now ain't they. Well no not ever body, he said, Not me. Then he give me a Smile and his Bandana to wipe my mouth off on and said Don't Worry I ain't gonna let no body Hang you for some thing you didn't never do. Or even for some thing you did do, he said. Like when you Robbed them two Old People.

WHAT'D I DO TO GET IN THIS FIX ANY HOW,

I said, Papa said. Well what was you doing just fore you got in this Fix, Calley said. I reckon that'll tell you How. Well I don't know, Papa said. Was it some thing Bad you done made you feel Bad bout doing it, Calley said. That's usually the Sign telling you you bout to fall off in a Deep Hole some wheres and maybe not never get out again. I didn't see no Sign, Papa said. Well No you don't see it so much as you hear it, Calley said. It's like a little Bell goes off way back there in your Head says Oh Hell No Mister Don't Do That Don't Do That. Well I don't know, Papa said. I can't think a'nothing cep maybe helping you break out a'the Jail House back in San Antoneya. Well no that wadn't no Bad Thing to do, Calley said, Must be some thing else you ain't remembered yet. Just don't never do nothing makes you feel Bad bout you self, he said, that's what that Little Bell way back in your Head is a'trying to tell you when it goes to Ringing. You done any thing here lately makes you feel Bad bout you self Mister Pearsall, Papa said. Well I don't know, he said, maybe just when I hit that Man over his Head for poking them poor Helpless Creatures with his Pointy Stick and then he died from it. You feel Bad bout that huh,

Papa said. Well no, Calley said, I feel Bad I didn't just go on and Shoot the Son of a Bitch cause they wanna Hang me for it any how. But maybe the best way to say what I'm a'trying to say, he said, is Just only do things make you feel Good bout doing and you won't never get you self in a Fix. They ain't never gonna Hang you, Papa said. You just a'Joking me now ain't you Mister Pearsall. Oh Yes Sir I'm only just a'Joking you he said. They ain't never nobody gonna Hang me I'm too Smart and too Funny for that ain't I. Well I don't know bout that but I don't believe o'Sheriff Pugh gonna let nobody Hang you anyhow Mister Pearsall cause a'how you tried to keep that man from a'Poking his Little Brother Johnny with that Stick remember. Yes Sir I do remember, Calley said, but o'Sheriff Pugh wadn't Sheriff a'San Antoneya Texas yet when I done that. What's that got to do with it, Papa said. Well I'm just not sure what he's gonna do now that he's changed Houses and is the new Sheriff, Calley said. We just gonna have to Watch and See when we get the Chance I reckon.

WE RODE ON IN TO GONZALES

in the early Afternoon, Papa said, and o'Calley stopped the first Man he seen on the Street and said You ain't seen Eurica Pearsall here some wheres today have you Sir and the Man said You might find her over at Conley's Arm and A Leg Store. She didn't hurt her self did she, Calley said. No Sir she married that Fella owns it, the Man said, and then Mister Pearsall touched his Finger to his John B and said Thank You Sir and we went on down the Street. Well, Calley said, Looks like my Sister didn't wait to hear her Husband Jack Ivy the Third is dead fore she went on and got her a'nother one. Least it's a Rich One this time. How you know that, Papa said. Well that Man said her new Husband owns The Arm and A Leg Store, Calley said, that's how. That's pretty much where ever body went to get they Missing Parts when they got Home from the War. Missing Parts, Papa said. Arms Legs Hands Ears Foots Things like that got shot off in the Fighting, Calley said. Oh they say People come from Miles all round cause they said o'Mister Conley could carve you a'new Leg so Good it could stand up and walk off by it's self Maybe even wiggle its Toes or Kick a'Cat. And then, Calley said, Mister Conley went to selling Glass Eyes and Teeth and got even Richer. At one time they say he was the Richest Man in Gonzales County and maybe he was I can't say for sure but I do know this, Mister Pearsall said, they was a'Time you always looked fore you shaked Hands with some body round here cause you just might find you was a'shaking Hands with some o'Piece a'Oak Wood Mister Conley carved a'Hand out of. He could do all that, Calley said, but he couldn't make you a new Nose to save his Life. Well wait a'minute I need to Say that over, he said, He could make you a new Nose he just couldn't get it to stay on you Face and People walked round with they Nose falling off in the Street all the time. Same thing with his Wood Ears, Calley said. You'd see some body reach up to scratch they Ear and Why it'd fall right off in they Hand and they'd go back and o'Mister Conley'd try to stick it back on for em and some times he could but most a'the Time he couldn't. So if you seen some body round here with they Nose or they Ear a'hanging off they Face well most likely that'd be some a'o'Man Conley's Work. But, he said, I wouldn't say nothing bout it if I was you cause most of em was in the War and ain't shy bout Shooting People for saying Things bout how they look.

WE WENT ON DOWN THE STREET, Papa said, and why they was a store had Wood Arms and Wood Legs and Wood Hands and whatnot a'hanging in the Winder and a sign writ in Wood Fingers that said CONLEY'S ARM AND A LEG STORE. This is it, Calley said, so we went on in and they was a Big Lady a'helping some Man try on a Glass Eye in the Mirra and the Man said This one don't match. My other one's Brown. Well the Lady said we all out a'Brown ones right now. If you don't like this Blue One you just gonna have to go on to some wheres else to get you a new Eye. They ain't no Some Wheres else to go and you know it the Man said. Well I can give you two Black Ones you go to Harping on me bout it like this Mister she said then looked in the Mirra and seen me and o'Calley a'standing there behind em. If you come to tell me o'Jack is Dead, she said, you bout a year and a'half too late you know it. I got busy on some thing else, Calley said. I wadn't sure how much you cared bout o'Jack any how Eurica. Yes Sir and I heared bout that Other Busy you been, she said. Now they's a Hand Bill out on you for it ain't they. Oh and that Man looked in the Mirra with his one Brown Eye to look at o'Calley and Calley said you

. . . they was a Big Lady a'helping some Man try on a Glass Eye in the Mirra and the Man said This one don't match

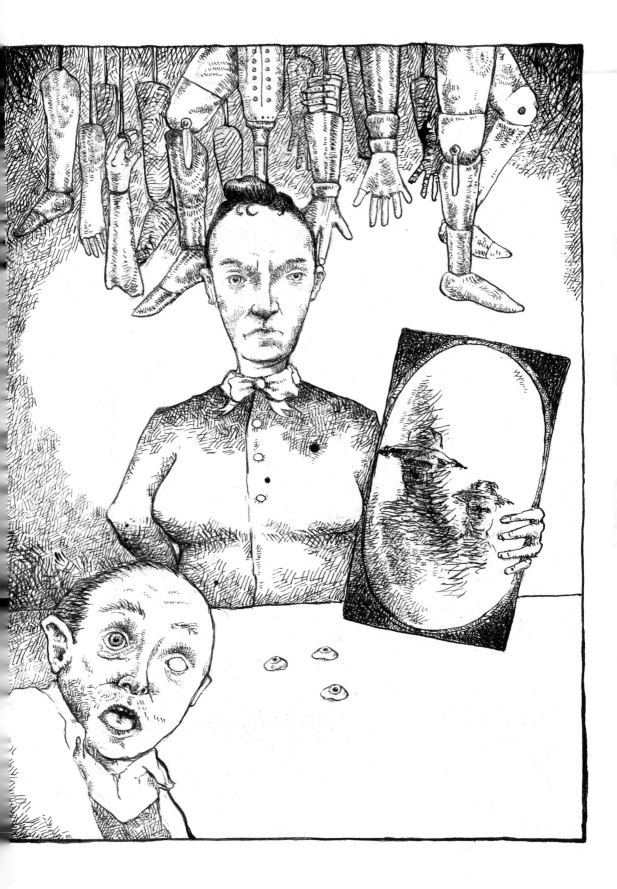

don't need to go spreading it round Eurica but now, Papa said, she seen me in the Mirra too and said And I reckon you that Boy Sin Nombre. They's a Reward out on you too ain't they Mister and Oh now that Man give me a Look too same as he did Calley and went to Blinking. No Ma'am I said, Papa said, I ain't no body. They say you Rob Old People too she said, How bout that. I know that been going round, Papa said, but no Ma'am I never. Your Momma and Daddy know you running round with a Out Law like o'Calley Pearsall here she said, No Ma'am they both Dead I said. Well I'm sorry to hear it, Eurica said, I wouldn't a'said nothing if I'd a'knowed that. Where's you new Husband at, Calley said. He ain't up and died too like all them others has he. No he's back in the Back some wheres a'carving out a'Arm for somebody lost one in the Saw Mill last year and been a'saving up his Money ever since to get him a new one. Well I reckon we got to get on now Eurica, Calley said. I just wanted to make sure you knowed bout o'Jack. Ever body in the whole County knowed o'Jack was Dead, she said, it wadn't never no Secret. Well I didn't know that, Calley said. You could a'saved you self the Trip if you had, she said. Well I just wanted to say Hello any how Eurica its been so long. Hello she said. Hello Calley said and then, Papa said, Eurica said Good Bye and Calley said Good Bye and we went on out Conley's Arm and A Leg Store like we hadn't never even been there in the First Place.

I GRABBED O'FRITZ UP, Papa said, and we rode on off from Conley's Arm and A Leg Store, and o'Calley went to Laughing bout some thing or other and just couldn't Quit. You gonna Laugh you self right off o'Firefoot there if you ain't careful Mister Pearsall I said, Papa said. I know it, Calley said, But I was just remembering this o'Story they usted to tell bout o'Man Conley and his Arm and A Leg Store is all. Yes Sir, Papa said. Well I ain't never heared it. Well Calley said, they was this o'Smarty Pants went in there one day and says I'm a'looking for me a new Wood Pecker. The one I got don't work no more, he said. You got any. And o'Man Conley says Well just the one but I'm a'using it my self. Oh and then o'Calley all but come a'part a'Laughing bout it all over again. Just the One o'Man Conley said, Calley said. Just the One but I'm a'using it my self. Now don't that just tickle your o'Funny Bone he said. Don't it.

That ain't Nice is it Mister Pearsall, Papa said. Well most things make you Laugh ain't Nice, Calley said. Tell me some thing Nice makes you Laugh Mister. But I couldn't think a'nothing right then, Papa said, but it didn't matter any how cause right then that Man a'trying to buy him a Glass Eye come a'running out Conley's Arm and A Leg Store and run cross the street and in the Sheriff's Office. Well I reckon we got my Sister Eurica and her Big Fat Mouth to thank for that, Calley said. Now ever god dam Wood Pecker in Gonzales County gonna be after us ain't they. And Oh then, Papa said, Why o'Calley just went to Laughing bout what he just said his self and I couldn't help it and went to Laughing my self and then he said, even o'Fritz went a'going Heh Heh Heh and we pushed our John Bs down on our Heads and give our Horses our Heels and lit a'shuck on out a'Gonzales Texas even if we was still just a'Laughing a'way at all the Funny Things happened to us when we was there.

We WADN'T BUT BOUT A MILE OUT

a'Gonzales, Papa said, when o'Calley dryed up his Laughing and said Don't look now but I think they's two Men a'follering us. So, Papa said, I looked back behind us and Oh Yes Sir they was two Men a'follering us a'Horseback just like he said. You think it's the Sheriff a'Gonzales County and that Man from in The Arm and A Leg Store, Papa said. I don't know, they just walking long same as us, Calley said, I can't tell they a'Chasing us or just out for a Ride. Here let's go this way, he said, and turned o'Firefoot a different Way and I did Sister the same Way. But them Two Men did the same xact thing, Papa said, and then Calley turned in a'nother Direction and I did too and Yes Sir them Two follered right a'long behind same as before but now o'Fritz went to low Growling bout it. Fritz don't like it them two a'follering us like this does he, Calley said. And I don't neither he said. Wonder why they ain't Shooting at us if they wanting the Reward. I think I know the one there on that Sorrel Horse, Papa said, but I don't know where from. Well Yes now that you mention it, Calley said, they both look a'little Familiar don't they. Oh and then O'Calley pulled out his big o'Pistola and said You stay here, I'm gonna go see. No Sir I ain't a'staying no wheres Mister Pearsall, Papa said, I'm a'going with you and when we turned our Horses to go see who it was

49

a'follering us why they both just stopped Dead in they Tracks and set there. Careful, Calley said, this might could be a Trick. You and Fritz stay back behind me. Then, Papa said, o'Calley pointed his o'Pistola at em and hollered Put your Hands up you SonsaBitches fore I Pop a'Cap on you. Why the god dam Hell you a'follering us any how, he said, We ain't that Pretty. But No, Papa said, they just set there quiet as a little Mouse and didn't say nothing back. Brave SonsaBitches I'll say that for em, Calley said. Here me a'pointing a'Pistola at em and they just a'setting there like they ain't got a Worry in the World. Oh and then, Papa said, Why them two come a'riding they Horses right at us. Uh Oh, Calley said, I believe they wanna Fight. Well come on then you SonsaBitches, he hollered, we gonna Whup you to a Fare-Thee-Well and send you back Home to you o'Momma but No, Papa said, they didn't care a'Lick and just kep on a'coming on. Maybe they ain't so much Brave as they are just plain Stupid, Calley said, then cocked his big o'Pistola back to Shoot if he had to. But right then, Papa said, I seen who it was and said Don't Shoot Mister Pearsall its them Two Robbers shot and killed each other back on the San Marcos River last night and then we tyed em on they Horses like that and let em go. Remember. Well they come close to getting they self Shot to Death all over a'gain, Calley said. I hope they know that he said then uncocked his big o'Pistola and put it back down his Pants but Oh, Papa said, Mister Pearsall hadn't no moren done that and of a sudden here come the Sheriff a'Gonzales County and a'Bunch a'other Men in a Posse just a'Hollering and a'Shooting at us and we give our Horses our Heels and run on off fast we could go and Oh then, Papa said, I looked over and Why o'Big Nose and Little Ears both went a'Running right on pass us like they Pants was on Fire and just a'Grinning bout it even if they was both already Dead and Gone.

*O*H ALL FOUR A'US DID RUN, Papa said, but the Sheriff a'Gonzales County and all his Men stayed right close on our Heel to where it looked like they was gonna run us all the way to Georgia and back. Then, he said, we seen this Fork in the Road a'coming up and o'Calley hollered Stay with Me Mister Stay with Me and then in a minute he had us running in a cluster with them two Dead Men running just close as we could get em to run and all this whole time the Sheriff a'Gonzales County and his Men was Catching Up Catching Up Catching Up not no moren a'Whisker back now but then we come to that Fork in the Road and when we did, Papa said, why o'Calley of a sudden reached over and give Sister a yank on the Rein to foller him and took us on the Left Fork while o'Big Nose and Little Ears went on the Right Fork and so did the Sheriff a'Gonzales County and all his Men right after em just a'Shooting and a'Hollering at em to Stop Stop Stop you SonsaBitches Stop Stop Stop but No, Papa said, them two Dead Men was already way on down the Road by now and we run a'nother mile or two then pulled our Horses up to catch they breath and take a'little Rest our self. You know what that was don't you, Mister Pearsall said. Well, Papa said, I reckon it was the Sheriff and all his Men a'wanting to catch us was What it was wadn't it. No Sir it was the Rest a'our god dam Life was What it was, o'Calley said. Ever day's gonna be just like this One here and then the next Day after this gonna be just like it too. Then, Papa said, he went to twirling his spur Ching e Ching e Ching-ChingChing and give me this Look had a Sadness and a Worry in it and said we Wanted Men now Mister and if they catch us they gonna Hang us both from the same Limb. That don't bother me, Papa said, If I'm a'gonna Hang I wanna Hang on the same Limb with you Mister Pearsall. No No, Calley said, the Idea is we don't never want em to catch us in the First Place. That way they can't never Hang us, he said. You need to look at the Pickle we in long range Mister. How we gonna keep em from catching us Mister Pearsall I said, Papa said. Well we just ain't gonna be no wheres round here for em to catch is How. Where you figgur we gonna go, Papa said. Well, Calley said, they's a Old Mexico and they's a New Mexico and I reckon one or the other's gonna be just right for us. What bout Texas, Papa said. You ain't saying Texas ain't gonna be our Home no more are you Mister Pearsall. I'm saying I don't never want you to Hang is what I'm a'saying and if we got to vacate Texas to save your Life and Mine then I say A'way we go Amigo. What bout Annie and Pela Rosa, Papa said. O'Calley shook his Head then, Papa said, and said I'm thinking maybe we oughta sneak back in San Antoneya and see what they got to Say bout it. Ain't that scarey, Papa said. Which one, o'Calley said, Sneaking back in San Antoneya or Telling the Ladies bout us maybe Leaving Texas forever.

said and off we did go to San Antoneya where we already was just a few days a'go but now you could tell we was even more Wanted Men'n we ever was before cause, Papa said, they was Wanted Signs bout us up on ever Tree in the Woods and ever Post on the Fence. Maybe we ought a'just writ our Ladies a Letter and go on to Mexico, Calley said. Oh Boy Hidy, Papa said, I didn't like it neither but my Feelings for Annie was getting such I'd bout risk any thing to See her just one more time fore me and o'Calley moved on off some wheres may be for the rest a'our Life. Least we know right where to go to find em, I said, it ain't like we got to go up and down the Street a'knocking on Doors to see if they Live there. And another thing, Calley said, is we gotta sneak in there to San Antoneya at Night to where can't no body see us any how in the Dark. Won't be no hardern skipping a Rock cross the Creek the way I see it he said. So, Papa said, we rode on in to San Antoneya that Night and then we put our John Bs over our Hearts cause we come a'riding pass the Alamo and Oh that Hanging Stand was still a'standing there ready for some body to put they Neck in the Noose and drop down out the Bottom. Well least I ain't a'Hanging there Tonight, Calley said, I reckon I got you to Thank for that Amigo. That's okay Mister Pearsall, Papa said, I was glad to do it. Course now, o'Calley said, they a'wanting to Hang you for it too. Oh and that give me a'little Chill, Papa said, cause they was so many People walking round there might could hear us a'talking and I said Not So Loud Not So Loud Mister Pearsall and then I seen all them Shimmery People a'going from one Person to a'nother and a'Whispering some thing in they Ear like that other Time to tell em what they needed to know but just wadn't able to tell they self. Them Shimmery People is all over the Place tonight you know it I said, Papa said. I don't see a'One, Calley said, but I believe any thing you say bout it. Well they's one over there Whispered in my Ear that Night we was all here together, Papa said, fore you killed that Man. I didn't never mean to kill him, Calley said, I just lost my Temper and give him a Lick for poking them poor Creatures like that and he Died from it. Yes Sir well that's what I meant Mister Pearsall, Papa said. You don't mind me and o'Fritz gonna go over there and see if he got any thing else to Say to me tonight. Yes Sir you just go on, Calley said. Me and o'Firefoot gonna just take us a'little Rest our self and then, Papa said, o'Calley climbed off Firefoot and set down on a Bench there in front a'that Hanging Stand and me and o'Fritz went a'riding over to that o'Shimmery Man I knowed from the Last Time I was here but Oh he seen me coming and said I wadn't never Here and now I'm Gone. Then, Papa said, he ducked down behind a'Bench to where he thought couldn't no body see him But its hard to Hide when you're a'Shimmering in the Dark like that.

I HEELED SISTER ON OVER THERE, Papa said, and said Why you a'hiding from me like this Mister I ain't never done nothing to you. I ain't hiding from you he said, I'm a'hiding from all them others round here that was in the Fight with the Mexkins here at the Alamo that time. You mean when they kilt ever Last Man I said, Papa said. That's Why I'm a'hiding, the Man said, they didn't kill me cause I run out the Back Door when the Mexkins come a'Hollering and a'Shooting and a'Stabbing up over the Wall at us. You went Yeller huh, Papa said, that what you a'saying bout you self huh Mister. Well I Run, the Shimmery Man said, you call it what you want to. Well what you call it Mister, Papa said. I reckon I call it Yeller too, he said then went to Crying bout it. Course I didn't get but maybe a'mile or two a'way from here when I come cross this Mexkin a'Running off from the Mexkin side a'the Fight and we just stood there a'Looking at each other cause we both Knowed the other one done turned Yeller his self but it's one Thing to know you turned Yeller you self and it's a whole nother Thing for you to know somebody else knows you turned Yeller too, the Man said, and couldn't neither one a'us a'bide that So of a sudden wadn't neither one a'us Scared a'nothing in this o'World moren we was Scared a'some body else a'Knowing we was Cowards and Oh then we went to Hollering and a'Shooting at one a'nother to keep our Secret hid but then my Lead Ball hit him in his Head and his Lead Ball hit me some wheres and we both dropped down Dead on the Ground and then I come a'Shimmering up out my Body and I thought Oh Good I'm Dead now and ain't no body ever gonna know I'm Yeller but then he said here come all these other Shimmery Men was killed back at the Alamo just a minute ago and one of em said Where was you in the Fight and I said Why I was right there on the Wall beside you just a'Shooting a'way like ever body else was and then a'nother one of em said No you wadn't You are a Black Lyer and a

53

god dam Yeller Belly Son of a Bitch to Boot ain't you. And then they left me all by my self, the Shimmery Man said, and that Mexkin I shot in his Head come a'Shimmering over from out his body and we both give each other a Hug and Oh just went to Crying cause now we was so Sorry we turned Yeller when our Friends needed us so Bad. And then, Papa said, the Man said we couldn't tolerate what we done and run on back to the Fight and tried to Jump back in Somebody's Body where they Jumped out from but No you just can't do it if you was already Dead like we was and I been here ever since And so has he, he said, then pointed over there cross the Plaza to where that Shimmery Mexkin Man was a'Whispering in Some body's Ear. So the Yeller didn't come off even if yall was Dead huh, Papa said. No Sir the Shimmery Man said. You ain't never shed a'nothing Good or Bad you ever done when you was over here in your Life. But, he said, the Good Thing is you always got the Chance to come on back over and make it Right if what you done wadn't too Bad in the First Place. Yes Sir, Papa said, that's when they go to Counting up your Black and White Dominoes on you ain't it. They what, the Shimmery Man said, And who's this They you a'talking bout here.

YOU MEAN WHEN YOU GOT KILT, Papa said, them Seven Old Men didn't set you down at a Table and go to Counting up your Dominoes for you. What Dominoes, the Shimmery Man said, I ain't got no Dominoes. Yes Sir you got White ones for all the Good Things you done in your Life and Black ones for all the Bad Things you done, Papa said. That's how it works. Well didn't no body never tell me nothing bout it, he said. That ain't Fair is it. Maybe they just waiting to tell you when they find you, Papa said. Well I been right here the Whole Time since I Died, the Man said, what they want me to do Stand Up and Holler I'm here I'm here I'm here. If you ask me, Papa said, you ain't much of a'Yeller Belly if you'd do that. Why'd you run out the Back Door any how. I didn't want no body to Shoot me is Why, the Shimmery Man said. You was sposted to be fighting for Texas like ever body else, Papa said, didn't that mean nothing to you. How was I gonna fight for Texas if they Kilt me. No Sir, he said, I figgured it was Better to make a Good Run'n a Bad Stand and I'd do my Fighting some wheres else on down the Road when they wadn't so many

Mexkins a'Shooting at me. Well now I don't know if you was a Yeller Belly or not, Papa said. Well if it makes you feel better, the Man said, I shot and Kilt that Skinny Mexkin right yonder then he grinned and waved to that Skinny o'Mexkin a'Shimmering over there by the Hanging Stand. Course, he said, he Kilt me right back for it didn't he and so wadn't much come of it one way or a'nother was it. My Gran Daddy Andrew and his Daddy John was both in the Fight over at San Hacinto, Papa said. You ain't saying nothing Bad bout them for Fighting are you Mister. I don't know what you could do bout it even if I was, he said, I'm already Dead if you was planning on Shooting me for it. I think you need to go talk to them Seven Old Men I was talking bout here a'minute ago, Papa said, I bet they can tell you what you oughta do next. I ain't going no wheres, the Shimmery Man said, I run off from here one time and I ain't never gonna Run off from here again. You ain't planning on just staying here til Kingdom Come are you, Papa said. I don't know Why Not he said Ever body round here already knows I'm a Coward ever wheres else I go. What I hear is you can get you a New Life and set it Right if you wadn't too Bad in your Old One. You talking bout them Old Men adding up my Black and White Dominoes again ain't you, he said. Yes Sir that's how it works, Papa said, far as I know. He set down then, Papa said, and said Oh I wouldn't even know where to look for em Mister and I said My o'Amigo Calley Pearsall used to say What Ever you a'Looking for in this World is out there in the World some wheres a'Looking for you too. You just got to Look and see if they's any body a'Looking for you. And then, Papa said, he went to Looking round and Oh of a sudden his Eyes got big and round on him and he said Is that them Old Men you a'talking bout Shimmering round that Table over there with they Dominoes and I looked, Papa said, and Yes Sir it was. See what I tole you I said. Oh he shaked his Head then and said I don't know I wanna go over there or not. You mean you just Happy being a Coward til Kingdom Come I said. He thought bout it a'minute, Papa said, then he waved to his Mexkin Friend that he killed to come on and they both went over there and set down at the Table with them Seven Old Men and it looked to me, he said, like them Old Men was glad to see em cause they give em each one a'Pet on they Head and started passing out White Dominoes for all the Good Things they done in they Life but not so many Black Ones for all the Bad Things.

AND THEN,

Papa said, Calley come over and said Who was you talking to over here and I pointed to where them two Cowards went to set down with them Seven Old Men but now, Papa said, they wadn't no body there no more. They ain't there no more, Papa said, they must a'gone on to some wheres else. We need to get on our self here in a minute if we gonna sneak in a Visit with the Ladies over at Senyora Garza's Place you know it. Yes Sir, Papa said. How we gonna do that. I been thinking bout it, Calley said, I reckon Best way is to send o'Fritz in there by his self to let em Know we in Town and then let em Sneak out to see us. How bout that, he said. Yes Sir I like that, I said, then we went over there cross the Street from Senyora Garza's Place and why there was o'Possum and Johnny and that poor Little o'One Eyed Bear a'setting out front on the Board Walk and now Johnny was a'wearing him a new Suit a'Clothes with a Watch Chain a'hanging out his Pocket and course a'John B Stetson Hat from down the Street at the Joske Brother Store. Fritz I said, Papa said, don't stop to visit just go on in there and let Annie and Pela Rosa know we in Town and wanna see em okay. But Fritz just give me a little Grin and run right on cross the Street and started sniffing on o'Possum's Hiney and ever thing else I tole him not to do and Oh then o'Possum and Johnny and that Little o'One Eyed Bear all three went to Howling and Carrying on loud as they could cause they was so glad to see o'Fritz after so long a Time and next thing here come the People out a'Senyora Garza's Place to see what was a'going on and Annie and Pela Rosa was there with em and Oh so was o'Sheriff Pugh and he put his Hand on his Pistol down there in his Pants cause he knowed if Fritz was there Why so was me and o'Calley too. Then he reached his Foot out and stepped on Fritz' Tail and Oh Fritz Hollered it hurt so Bad and run right on back cross the Street to where me and Calley was a'hiding in the Shadow to get him a Pet or maybe to give us a Bite cause we was the Ones sent him over there in the First Place. Any how, Papa said, here come o'Sheriff Pugh right behind him with his Pistol drawed. Hands Up Hands Up, he said, You Boys is Under Arrest for Murder and Jail Break and they ain't no Help for you now. But then here come o'Possum and Johnny and that poor Little o'One Eyed Bear a'running cross the Street cause o'Calley was the One stopped Sheriff Highschoote's Little Brother from poking em with that Sharp Stick and he always been they Friend before and, Papa said, they wadn't bout to let no Harm come to him now if they could help it.

give me and Calley both a good Poke in our Belly with his Pistol, Papa said, and said Git on over there to the Jail House and I mean Right Now you SonsaBitches but Johnny come a'hobbling over and wrapped his little Fins round his Big Brothers Legs and went to shaking his Head No No No No No No but, Papa said, Sheriff Pugh was gonna do it any how and give Johnny a Hard Push out the way and said Git off me Johnny or I will just suren Hell give you a Knot on your god dam Head biggern a Water Melon you self but then o'Possum went after Sheriff Pugh's Leg with his Teeth and that poor Little o'One Eyed Bear give the Sheriff a Bear Hug that took him to the Ground and Sheriff Pugh tried to shoot him Dead for it but No he missed and shot Pela Rosa in sted when she was just running up from Senyora Garza's Place and Oh, Papa said, Oh Calley let out a Scream sounded like the End of the World and run over there to hold his Sweet Heart in his Arm and the last thing she ever said in this World was I'll Wait for You. Then her Eyes give him one Last Look and rolled back in her head and Pela Rosa was Gone Gone Gone Gone For Ever and me and Calley and Annie all three a'us bout come a'part bout it, Papa said, and didn't have no Idea what to do next but Annie give me a Hug and a Push and said Yall got to Go fore they Blame you for this too. But, Papa said, o'Calley wadn't having it that way and pulled his big o'Pistola out his Pants and went over there his Eyes all Bugged out and just a'Crying and put the Bullet End up gainst the side a'o'Sheriff Pugh's Head and cocked the Hammer Back far as it'd go and they wadn't no doubt in all the World Mister but what he was gonna blow o'Sheriff Pugh's Brains right out the other side a'his Head but just when he was bout to pull the Trigger why he seen o'Johnny just a'Crying and a'Shaking his Head No No No Oh Please No cause even if he didn't know xactly what was a'going on here he knowed his Big Brother was bout to get his head blowed off and he Loved him so much and he just kept a'shaking his Head No No No Oh No No No and o'Calley just couldn't let his self make o'Johnny a Orphan a'gain like he always been fore his Big Brother come to Town and bought him a new Suit a'Clothes and a John B Stetson Hat and whatnot over at the Joske Brother Store. So, Papa said, o'Calley blowed Sheriff Pugh's Ear off his Head for him in sted so he'd always remember what a Bad thing he done to Pela Rosa ever time he went to scratch his Ear. Oh and then the People did run a'way from there cause the Sheriff's Ear went a'flying off in ever which Direction, Papa said, and on them too.

MY O'AMIGO GATHERED HIS PELA ROSA

up in his Arm then and rode off on Firefoot with me and Annie and Fritz on Sister and then o'Possum and Johnny and that poor Little o'One Eyed Bear all come a'follering long behind on Foot, Papa said, and then here come Senyora Garza and a'lot a'other People used to like to hear Pela sing and watch her Dance on the Bar there in Senyora Garza's Place and Oh, Papa said, we went all the way up there cross the San Antoneya River to that Place where we buried Little Missey's o'Blind Panther that day long time a'go after all them Men shot and killed him. Oh it was a Sad Day, Papa said, a Sad Sad Day and ever body Cried bout it and just couldn't stop Crying even when me and o'Calley dropped the last shovel a'dirt down on Pela to cover her up there in that Hole we digged for her to Sleep in forever. I Loved her, Calley said. I Loved her with all my Heart and now it's Broke in Two and ain't never gonna grow back together ever a'gain. Then, Papa said, Calley blowed Pela Rosa a Last Kiss there under the dirt and put his John B back on his Head and heeled o'Firefoot on off and I said to Annie I got to go with him Annie he's my Friend and she said We sure having a Hard Time being Together ain't we and I said Yes I know it but I got to go any how Annie. And then, he said, me and o'Fritz rode on off after Calley and when I looked back I seen o'Possum and Johnny and that poor Little o'One Eyed Bear a'standing there with Annie and Oh they was all just a'Crying to where it made you Cry some more you self just to see it.

CALLEY DIDN'T SAY NOTHING,

Papa said, til we was Way Way a'Way from there then he pulled Firefoot up and said I am for dam sure a Out Law now and they will come a'Day that One Eared Sheriff Simon Pugh will Catch me and Hang me but when that Day comes, he said, I don't want you no wheres round to see it. So, he said, Shake my Hand Adios Amigo and go on back to your Sweet Heart in San Antoneya and sneak off with her to some wheres else where that Sheriff won't never find you. No Sir Mister Pearsall I said, Papa said. I can't do that. Well you just sure as god dam Hell can do that, Calley said. Now turn o'Sister round and give her you Heels and don't never look back to see where I gone. No Sir, Papa said. No Sir. Yes Sir, o'Calley said. Yes Sir. No Sir No Sir,

Then her Eyes give him one Last Look and rolled back in her head and Pela Rosa was Gone Gone Gone Gone For Ever . . .

Papa said, I ain't a'gonna do it and you can't make me. Why you bucking me like this, Calley said, What the Hell's come over you. I'm fraid you riding on the Devil's Fork now Mister Pearsall, Papa said, and gonna go out there some wheres and try to get you self Kilt cause you don't care bout Living no more now that Miss Pela's gone, Papa said, Ain't that right. Oh he give me a Look then like I just seen through his Trick and said You getting Smart here in your Old Age ain't you Mister. I ain't Leaving you Mister Pearsall, Papa said. I might not know ever thing they is to know in the World but I know I ain't a'Leaving you. O'Calley cocked his Boot up on a knee then and went to Twirling his spur Ching e Ching e ChingChingChing and said Even if I was to say Okay I don't believe you and o'Sister there could Keep Up with us moren a day or two at the Most any how. Well you might be Right Mister Pearsall, Papa said. And you might be Wrong. I reckon we just gonna have to see which one ain't we. And then, he said, o'Calley give me a Look for my Sass and touched his Heel to Firefoot and rode on off with me and Sister and o'Fritz a'follering long behind like I tole him we was gonna do so I hollered See There Mister Pearsall you can't no more get a'way from me'n you can you own Shadow.

*B*UT OH YES HE COULD, Papa said, and by Sun Down he wadn't no wheres in the Country you could see. Where'd he go Fritz, I said, but Fritz didn't have no more Idea bout it'n me and I didn't even ask Sister cause I knowed she didn't know nothing neither. We got to find him I tole em, Papa said. If we don't find him he's gonna get his self Kilt some wheres and be glad of it. So the Moon come Up and the Stars come Out and we just kep a'Looking ever which way we could but No didn't see no sign a'nobody but then we crossed this little Creek and way off up yonder some body had em a Camp Fire a'going and when we got up there to see we seen a'Pan a'Beans and a note under a Rock said Go on back Home to your Sweet Heart. This is the last a'my Beans. Your Amigo Calley Pearsall. But course we didn't have no Idea where he went and me and o'Fritz and Sister worried our self to Sleep bout it. But next Morning when I waked up why there was Mister Pegleg a'setting right side me just a'Shimmering like ever body Dead always Shimmers once they Dead. You got some thing to tell me ain't you Mister Pegleg I said, Papa said, and Mister Pegleg give me a pull on my sleeve to foller and not just set there like a Knot on a Log. So me and Fritz et the Beans and Sister et her some Grass and a'way we went a'follering Mister Pegleg out a'cross the Country and Oh, Papa said, we went through Cactuses and Mesquites and up Hills and down Canyons and cross some body's Corn Field and we did it for Days and Days and then some more Days and then some more Days after that cause o'Mister Pegleg just wouldn't quit. Course, Papa said, he was Dead and didn't need nothing to eat but we had to cook Cactus Leaves and pick Berrys or we'd a'all starved to Death and no body the wiser. And one time we got so Hungry I went and stole a Chicken out from off the Roost in some body's Hen House and me and o'Fritz eat it right up even if I did feel Bad bout stealing it but that's what happens if you Hungry nough and we was. But still no Sign a'o'Calley and I didn't have no Idea where we was neither but that didn't stop us and On and On and On and On we went for Weeks now I reckon and Sister never complained a'step and she was the one doing most a'the Walking while I was doing most a'the Riding and o'Fritz was pretty much doing all the Napping. But still no Sign a'o'Calley and Oh I was getting fraid may be he run cross some body shot and killed him like he wanted em to. But then this one day, Papa said, we was follering Mister Pegleg through some Town and why right up yonder o'Firefoot was a'standing at the Hitching Post in front a'this Saloon and Oh they was People running out the Door like they Pants was on Fire.

$\mathcal{S}$O I RUN ON UP THERE

quick's I could, Papa said, and ooched my way tween some body's Legs til I was in there and Oh then I seen o'Calley and this other Man a'setting at a table a'giving each other the Snake Eyes and a'pointing they Pistols at one another. You are bout the Ugliest Son of a Bitch I ever did see in my Life Mister, Calley said, I don't believe I ever seen no Uglier less it was may be your Ugly o'Wife or your Little Chilrens one. Oh that other Man squeezed his Pistol like he was gonna shoot, Papa said, but o'Calley just give him a Smile and said I believe I'd Shoot any Man ever said some thing like that to me bout my Ugly Wife and Ugly Little Chilrens. I'm that way my self the

Man said, Papa said, and cocked his Pistol back. You gonna Shoot me for it now huh, Calley said. I might, the Man said, I'm thinking bout it and Oh his Hand just went to Shaking like a Leaf. You're Ugly too and here's a'nother thing bout you Mister, Calley said, you ain't got nough Ass in your Britches to pull that Trigger on me. But, Papa said, I seen o'Calley was Dead Wrong bout that and that Man was sure nough bout to pull the Trigger on him so I let out a Holler and said Oh Please don't shoot my Daddy Mister Please Please Please Don't and then o'Fritz run over there and jumped up in Calley's lap and went to Licking on his Face and Calley come all a'part and put his Head down on the table and went to Crying. What's wrong with him, the Man said, he don't look so Mean now. He wadn't never really gonna Shoot you, Papa said, He was just looking for some body to Shoot him cause he been so Sad here lately bout losing his Sweet Heart. Oh the Man said, Papa said, then he give o'Calley a'Pet on his Back and said I'm sorry Mister truly I am and them other Men in there went over there and give Calley Pets too like they was old Friends cause they wadn't a'one of em hadn't at one time or a'nother in they Life lost em a Sweet Heart they self and knowed just xactly how it felt when you did. And I reckon it was then, Papa said, I come to know Love could pull you a'part or put you back together again either one. Just depended, he said, on if they was other People round who been through the same thing and wadn't Shy bout showing you You wadn't never really just all a'lone in the World.

*I*T TOOK SOME DOING,

Papa said, but me and that Man got o'Calley out side the Saloon and up on o'Firefoot. He's welcome to come stay at my Place a day or two if he wants to, the Man said. I admit my Wife is Ugly but not so Ugly as my Brother's. No Sir thank you Sir I said, Papa said, I better get him on back up the Country where he come from so he don't take a'nother notion to put his self in Harm. Well you always Welcome but be careful as you go cause I know the Sheriff a'San Antoneya is a'looking for some body like yall and they's People round here'd Shoot you for the Money. Yes Sir I know it, Papa said, but we didn't never do nothing to deserve such a thing that I know of. I believe you, the Man said, but some time they's People got a Gun and just like to Scratch

. . . I seen o'Calley and this other Man a'setting at a table a'giving each other the Snake Eyes and a'pointing they Pistols at one another.

63

they Itch to Shoot some body and don't care a'Lick you done any thing Bad or not. I know you right bout that Mister, Papa said, I seen it my self one or two times. Then the man reached up his Hand to Calley and said Good to meet you Mister I'm glad we didn't Shoot one a'nother ain't you and Calley said No Sir I ain't. Then he give o'Firefoot his Heel and rode on off down the Street and I give the Man a'Tip a'my John B to say Thank You Mister and me and o'Fritz and Sister rode on after him and when we catched up I said You got any Idea where you a'going now Mister Pearsall and he said No I ain't and I don't reckon I ever will Know again in my Life neither. Well then I said, Papa said, you just as well come long with me cause I know xactly where I'm a'going. And where's that Calley said and I said Well I reckon you just gonna have to watch and see for you self you wanna find out. What if I don't wanna Find Out he said. What bout that. Well is that what you a'saying Mister Pearsall, Papa said. You a'saying you got some place else you wanna go in sted. O'Calley looked all round at the World then, Papa said, and you never seen no body more lostern him in you whole Life. I don't know nothing he said. In Fact I don't believe I'm ever gonna Know any thing at all from here on out. Well they's only one thing they is to Know right now, Papa said, and that's that we a'going some wheres to start us a whole New Life where you ain't always out there a'trying to get some body to Shoot you Dead. How you like that Mister Pearsall I said and he said Not worth a god dam Mister. So we just kep a'going and I didn't say no more bout it.

O'CALLEY DIDN'T SAY MUCH A'NOTHING the first three four days we was a'riding a'way from there, Papa said, and at night o'Fritz'd go over there and give him a'Lick cross his Face to try to Spunk him up some but No, he said, ever time o'Fritz'd go to give him a Kiss why o'Calley'd push him a'way and say Git Dog Git Git Git I don't want no Kiss but one day bout a week later, Papa said, o'Calley looked over at o'Fritz a'riding long there on my Lap and said Fritz you wanna come over here and ride with me a'while and Fritz jumped right on over there to ride with him on o'Firefoot. I'm glad to see you Fritz, Calley said, I been a'missing you Amigo then he give him a Pet on his Head and some more all over and o'Fritz grinned over at me and went Heh Heh Heh like he had him a better

Life a'going now'n he ever had when he was a'riding with me. But it wadn't long after that, Papa said, and we started a'seeing all these Hand Bills ever wheres offering Money for some body to Catch or Shoot Calley Pearsall and the Boy Sin Nombre for they Crimes. We must be getting close to San Antoneya don't you reckon if they putting out Hand Bills like that round here, Papa said. Now that I boogered up o'Sheriff Pugh's Ear for him like I did, Calley said, he gonna be putting out signs like that all the way to Georgia and back. So keep a Good Eye out, he said. I'm glad to hear you ain't wanting some body to Shoot you no more Mister Pearsall, Papa said. You ain't riding the Devil's Fork no more are you. Not less I'm still on it and can't get off I reckon he said but, Papa said, I could tell he was a little worried Was he still on the Devil's Fork or not. You keep a Good Eye out you self Mister Pearsall I said. It don't hurt for neither one a'us to be careful. But just when I said it, Papa said, we had to Duck down Quick cause right then o'Sheriff Pugh and his Men come a'riding by with some more Hand Bills bout us to nail up on Trees but now Sheriff Pugh'd growed his Hair Long and combed it all the way down over the side a'his Head to cover up his ugly o'Ear Hole that we seen when the Wind come up and blowed his Hair back. That Son of a Bitch ain't gonna Kiss no Babies a'looking like that is he, o'Calley said. I reckon his Chance to set in the Governor's Chair is all over now aint it. I didn't know he wanted to set in it, Papa said. Where'd you hear that. No I never, Calley said, I just reckon he's the kind a'Son of A Bitch who'd want to is all.

WE DODGED GOING THROUGH SAN ANTONEYA, Papa said, so wouldn't no body see us and Hang us from that Hanging Stand out there in front a'the Alamo but it bout Broke my Heart not to go say Hidy to Annie when we was so close by and o'Calley seen it on my Face. You a'missing your Sweet Heart ain't you, he said, and wish you could go over there and give her a Hug huh. I don't know I said, Papa said, I might be. But then I seen the look on his Face and I said I reckon you a'missing your Sweet Heart too ain't you Mister Pearsall but he couldn't answer me back, Papa said, cause it Hurt his Heart too Bad. Well I bet you was Glad to have your Sweet Heart when you did have her wadn't you Mister Pearsall, Papa said, ain't that Right and Oh it took him bout a'year to answer but when he did he said Yes Sir I was Glad to have my Sweet Heart I sure was. I was more Glad a'that'n any thing else in my whole Life. And still am by god he said. Well, Papa said, I reckon I carry the same thing round with me bout my Momma. It's Hard ain't it, Calley said. Might be harder if you didn't never have a'Sweet Heart you cared bout that much, huh, Papa said. I reckon that'd be Hard too don't you Mister Pearsall. I reckon so, o'Calley said, but I don't reckon it'd ever be Hard as having One and not having her no more then he give me a'little Smile but you could see they was Bad Bad Hurt in it. Where we a'going any how, he said, you ain't taking me in for the Reward Money are you Mister. Well if I did, Papa said, you reckon they'd give me the Reward Money for taking my self in too. I'm glad to hear you got your Funny Bone working again, Calley said, I been a'missing that here these last nine years or so. Well you ain't been so Funny you self here lately Mister Pearsall you know it, Papa said. They ain't been nothing much to be Funny bout that's why Calley said and I said I know it Mister Pearsall and I'm sorry I said any thing bout it. That's okay, Calley said, I reckon we can go us a'day or two without a'Laughing bout some thing huh. No Sir, Papa said, that's too long not to Laugh. Well then maybe just a day he said and I said No Sir that's too long too not to Laugh. Well then how long Not to Laugh is okay then he said A'half a'day and I said No Sir got to be lessen that. Lessen a'half a'day Not to Laugh, he said. Well god dam how bout just one minute then. A minute I said and o'Calley said Yes Sir just one minute Not to Laugh and then he went to Laughing and I said what you a'Laughing bout now and he said Nothing it's just that the Minute's up and it's Time to go a'Laughing a'gain and Oh, Papa said, then I went to Laughing too and we both started feeling Better bout things.

*W*E PASSED SAN ANTONEYA BY, Papa said, and went on and o'Calley said I been this way before Mister so you ain't Fooling me bout Where we a'going. Well name it then you know so much I said and o'Calley said we a'going to the Choats ain't we. Yes Sir, Papa said, Don't that make you Glad. What we gonna do at the Choats he said, Hide in the Barn or out in the Pasture some wheres so can't no body find us. Listen here, Calley said, that ain't no Life for a'Boy. It ain't no Life

66

for you neither Mister Pearsall, Papa said. I been thinking bout a'nother place ain't got all this Trouble comes with it. I ain't a Farmer if that's what you thinking, Calley said. I ain't a'gonna go round wearing Over Alls and cussing Bugs. It ain't so bad, Papa said, I done it my self when I was just a little Fella. No Sir not for me, Calley said, Thank You just the same Mister. You ain't saying you going back on the Devil's Fork a'gain are you I said and o'Calley said I ain't saying nothing cep I ain't gonna be no god dam Dirt Farmer. Well how bout we get us some Horses then and be Horse Traders in sted I said. Two things bout that, Calley said, Number One where we gonna get these Horses you a'talking bout here and Number Two even if we do get em where's our Ranch at to put em on. We catch em out a'the Cedar Brakes all up and down the Blanco River where they been a'hiding all this time like me and my mean o'Daddy used to do, Papa said. How bout that. Oh I could tell Calley kind a'liked the idea and cocked his Foot up on his Saddle Horn and went to twirling his spur Ching e Ching e ChingChingChing. Well that's True, he said, they's Horses all over the Place out there in the Brush long the River that run off from some body or other ain't they. Yes Sir we'd just have to Catch em is all and put em in the Pen, Papa said. What Pen's that you a'talking bout, Calley said. You got a Pen some wheres you ain't never tole me bout. I don't know I might have, Papa said, up there where I come from. You ain't talking bout your mean o'Daddy's Place are you. Yes Sir I might be, Papa said. You give your Half a'the Place to your Brother Herman that day don't you remember it, he said. You said you didn't want it no more and for him to just take it. Well I bet he ain't never done Nothing with it but just let it set there, Papa said. May be we could cut him in on the Money we gonna make off our Horses for the use a'the Place. Give you Brother Herman Money for not doing one god dam thing, Calley said. Yes Sir I reckon that'd suit him just Fine wouldn't it. I reckon you kind of a'Busness Man ain't you. Oh I bowed up at that, Papa said, and said Yes Sir I reckon I am if you say so. Then o'Calley give his Spur a'nother seven ten twirls Ching e Ching e ChingChingChing and said Hell why not. We both still young Men with a'lot a'Pepper in our Shaker ain't we. Yes Sir, Papa said, you and me huh Mister Pearsall. Why don't you just call me Calley from here on out if we gonna be Partners in the Horse Busness together. Okay Calley, Papa said, Thank you Mister Pearsall. Oh and then we Laughed bout me saying that and Shaked our Hand on it.

WE RODE ON UP TO THE CHOATS,

Papa said, and Oh they was People ever wheres you looked a'lot of em I seen fore on that Day o'Jeffey died in her Bed out there under the Tree. And right over there, he said, Bird was a'setting on Marcellus' Knee and answering Questions from People in o'Jeffey's voice but then she seen us through Bird's Eyes and said Yall just gonna have to get in Line and set tight a'minute. So, Papa said, we went over there and set on the Porch to wait a Turn and then here come Mister and Miz Choat out the House with some Grape Juice for the People but bout dropped it when they seen me and o'Calley a'setting there. Oh Lord, Miz Choat said, Oh Lord in Heaven then she come over there and give me and o'Fritz a'Hug and o'Calley a'little Pet on his cheek and said I was fraid they done Hanged you Mister Pearsall and he said No Ma'am not yet and she said Well we gotta see to it it's Not Never. Well don't go Biting off moren you can chew Miz Choat, Calley said. We going in the Horse Busness Miz Choat, Papa said, me and Calley. I don't know why Not, she said, Do you Mister Choat and Mister Choat said I never was much of a Horse Man my self but I made a pretty good Farmer. Yes you did Mister Choat, Miz Choat said, Yes Sir you sure did Mister Choat and give him a'Squeeze. Calley don't wanna be a Farmer, Papa said, and I'm pretty much the same way bout it my self. I hate grubbing them Mesquites I said. I know it, Mister Choat said, that'll bout Kill you won't it but it's some thing Fine and Wonderful to see a Seed you planted you self come a'sprouting up one morning in the Sun Shine and go to growing. I never get over it my self he said. I guess I just ain't Bent that way is all, Calley said. Well ever body to they own Likes I reckon, Miz Choat said, Course don't nobody ever ask what that might be for the Woman do they. Well Miz Choat, Calley said, you can throw in with us you wanna be a Horse Woman and we be Glad to have you. I bet you'd run for the Hills if I was to say Yes to that wouldn't you Mister Pearsall, Miz Choat said. But fore he could answer, Papa said, o'Marcellus hollered at me to come on it was bout my Turn so I went over there and give Marcellus a Hello Hug and Bird one too but what come out a'Bird's mouth was o'Jeffey a'saying You got company a'coming and I said Well who's that you talking bout there Miz Jeffey and she said Well turn round and look for you self You ain't blind are you. So I turned round, Papa said, and Why here come Annie and Johnny a'riding double on a Horse and o'Possum and that poor Little o'One Eyed Bear just a'follering long behind Happy as you Please.

Then Johnny come a'hobbling up just a'Smiling. Hello Johnny me and o'Calley said, Papa said, then shaked his little Fingers and give him a Smile back.

O'FRITZ RUN OVER THERE, Papa said, and went to trading Hiney Sniffs with o'Possum and then I jumped and run over there too quick's I could and Annie jumped down off that Horse and give me a Hug and wouldn't let go for nothing. You ain't never getting out my Sight a'gain Mister, she said, don't even think bout it. No I don't never want you out a'my Sight a'gain neither Annie, I said, cause I'd just have to come find you some wheres. Then Calley stepped up and Annie said that Sheriff in San Antoneya is a'looking for you for how Ugly you made him Look when you blowed his Ear off. Then Johnny come a'hobbling up just a'Smiling. Hello Johnny me and o'Calley said, Papa said, then shaked his little Fingers and give him a Smile back. He don't want no more to do with his Brother Sheriff Pugh cause a'how he Shot and Killed your Sweet Heart Pela Rosa Mister Pearsall, Annie said. So he's traveling with us now like in a Family and that Little o'One Eyed Bear too. It's like being in a Circus ain't it huh, Calley said, but Annie said No Sir it's a Family like I said it is Ain't you a'listening. Then, Papa said, Mister Choat stepped up with the Grape Juice and said Here don't yall want some Grape Juice after you long Ride and Johnny and that Little o'Bear each took em a big drink out the Pitchur and smacked they Lips Smack Smack Smack like that to where you couldn't help but Laugh bout it. Then, he said, Annie looked over there and seen Bird a'setting on Marcellus' knee and said Is o'Jeffey still a'talking out Little Bird's mouth like she started a'doing last time we was here. Yes she is, Miz Choat said, and people a'coming from all over to hear what she got to say to em from the Other Side like always. I might like to hear Some Thing my self, Annie said. Well you just gonna have to get in Line like ever body else and wait your Turn, Miz Choat said, o'Jeffey don't play no Favorites round here. So, Papa said, Annie took me by my Hand and pulled me over to the Back a'the Line to wait a Turn and then here come Johnny and that Little o'One Eyed Bear right long with us and then Fritz and o'Possum too. What you reckon she's gonna say to a One Eyed Bear, Annie said. I don't have no Idear, Papa said, I don't reckon he's gonna understand it what ever it is any how. And then Johnny went to flapping his little Arms he thought it was so Funny.

$\mathcal{B}$UT WHEN IT WAS ANNIE'S TURN,

Papa said, why o'Jeffey said No not her Him and Bird pointed at Johnny to show Who she was talking bout was Next and then, he said, o'Calley led Johnny up to the front a'the Line and o'Johnny stood there with this big o'Grin on his Face. You picked you a Hard Life this Time round you know it Mister, o'Jeffey said But, Papa said, Johnny just stood there a'Looking back at her like some o'Loonie out the Loonie Bin but then of a sudden he give her a little Wink but I couldn't tell was it on purpose or just a Fly went by. You ready for me now Ma'am, Annie said, but o'Jeffey looked up at me through Bird's Eyes in sted and said They's some body over here wants to wish you Good Luck with that Horse Busness you a'starting. Who is it I said, Papa said, It ain't my Momma is it. No Sir, she said, it's your Brother Herman is who it is. Well no Ma'am, Papa said, couldn't be my Brother Herman cause my Brother Herman ain't Dead. I don't believe I'd bet my Boots on that if I was you Mister, o'Jeffey said. And he says to say Hidy to you too Mister Pearsall she said then give o'Calley a'little Smile. We wadn't xactly Friends, Calley said. Last time I seen Herman I hit him in his Face for being Greedy and Rude. Well for ever Lick You give Some Body for what ever Reason You give it to em You gonna get a Lick back from some body else. That's how it works you know it, she said. Well Yes Ma'am Miz Jeffey I do know it, Calley said, but I didn't think that pertained when you in the Right. Who tole you You was in the Right when you give o'Herman a'Lick that day, o'Jeffey said, somebody just drop down out the Clouds and whisper it in your Ear when you wadn't looking. No Ma'am, Calley said, I reckon I just tole my self I was in the Right to give him that Lick cause I damn sure was. And Oh, Papa said, the Smoke was just a'coming out his Nose and Ears when he said it and then o'Jeffey said Wooo you got a Temper on you ain't you that's gonna be the First Thing you gonna have to go to School on once you get over here on my Side. Now go on a'way with you, she said, They's other people in the World got a Question. So, Papa said, we went on off but Annie was sorry bout it cause she didn't never get to ask her Question. Maybe she didn't give me no Question cause the Answer for it is too Bad for me to Hear, Annie said.

THAT EVENING WHEN EVER BODY

was gone out the yard back to they Home, Papa said, Miz Choat come over to me and said You that Boy they call Sin Nombre on the Hand Bills ain't You. Yes Ma'am I am but ain't no body knows what I look like enough to put the Budge on me. Well Mister Pearsall ain't that Lucky, she said, they know what he looks like. Ain't no body gonna even be able to see him once we get in the Horse Busness, Papa said. Tell him to grow him a big long Beard and a Mustache maybe wear a Patch over one Eye so won't no body never know him, she said. We'll get a'long, Papa said, I ain't too Scared bout it. Oh she give me a Knock on my Head for that and said Listen here Boy some thing Bad happen to you it'd just Break my o'Heart and Annie's too I reckon and then, Papa said, she pointed over to where Annie was holding Bird and showing him how to give that poor Little o'One Eyed Bear a'Pet while Fritz and o'Possum was a'waiting their Turn and Mister Choat was trying to show o'Johnny how to flip his Hat up in the Air and make it land on his Head but No he couldn't do it his self. Annie fits right in our Little Circus here don't she, Miz Choat said. You wanna make sure you don't never lose her you a'listening. Yes Ma'am, Papa said. To hear her tell it we gonna get Married some day. First Time I ever met her, Miz Choat said, I seen she had her Eye on You and that suits me fine. I wouldn't want some o'Bowleg Sheep Herder's Daughter to land on you. I don't even know no o'Bowleg Sheep Herder's Daughter Miz Choat, Papa said. Well they sneak up on you in the Night when you ain't looking and next thing you know they put on bout a'hunderd and two pounds and You can't even roll em off the Bed no more. Where you getting all this, Papa said, I never heared that. I just know things, she said. If you Smart as I think you are you'll listen to ever Word I say. Yes Ma'am Miz Choat, Papa said, I do. Well you better she said and give me a'nother little Knock on my Head and a Pet on my cheek. I'm sorry bout your Brother Herman, she said. Well, I said, I don't know that's True or Not what o'Jeffey said out Little Bird's mouth. Well if it ain't True, Miz Choat said, its gonna be the First Time some thing out her mouth wadn't True. And here's another thing, she said, Don't never ask her nothing you ain't sure you wanna know the Answer to.

# NEXT MORNING,

Papa said, we rode out for where I was borned and raised and I was mighty Scared a'what we was gonna find cause a'what o'Jeffey said bout my Brother Herman already being over there on the other side with her now. I'm Scared too, Annie said. Well they ain't nothing to do but go see, Calley said, then deal with it don't matter what it is. I'm sorry we wadn't better Friends, Papa said. I feel Bad bout that. No you was a good Brother, Calley said, I seen that my self. He couldn't a'ask for no better. Then Calley looked over there where Annie and Johnny was a'riding Double on her Horse and said Gonna be hard to be Married and be in the Horse Busness both at the same Time you know it. Well my Momma and Daddy done it, Papa said. Yes sir and you seen how that turned out didn't you, Calley said. Well who said we was getting Married now any how, Papa said. Don't nobody need to say it, Calley said, Womens just wanna get married is all Don't Matter what time a'Day or Night it is or if they Fourteen or Two Hunderd and Four. Well I'm sorry you lost Pela Rosa, Papa said. No Sir didn't lose her, Calley said then Petted his Heart. No Sir she's right in here. We Talk ever Night, he said, did you know that. No Sir I didn't, Papa said. What Yall talk bout. Well First Thing is bout how Sorry we are we ain't on the same Side no more he said and Wish we was. You mean You can hear each other a'talking back and forth like that through the Wall, Papa said. No it ain't xactly like that, Calley said. It's more like Hearing Thoughts. The more you was in Love when you was a'Live together, he said, the better you are at Hearing Thoughts when you Dead. You know a'lot bout a'lot a'things don't you Calley, Papa said. Yes Sir I do I sure do, he said, and I always have I reckon.

I KNOWED THEY WAS SOME THING WRONG

when I seen Old Karl's Money Box up side down out there in the Yard, Papa said, and if that wadn't nough to tell me the Front Door been kicked in to Boot. You better let me go see, Calley said, I wouldn't want you to see some body done some thing Bad to your Brother Herman in there but, Papa said, o'Fritz and Possum and that poor Little o'One Eyed Bear run on in there didn't matter me a'hollering No No No at em or not. You gonna have to teach em to mine Better here one a'these days you know it, Annie said. I don't believe even o'Genral Houston could teach em nothin, Papa said, they so onery ain't they. Then, he said, Me and Calley and Annie and Johnny went on in the House and Oh Papa said I was a'Scared to Death a'what we was a'gonna find but what we did find was some body or other had had em a Big Fight and knocked ever thing over and broke Dishes and spilt the Sugar and all the Flower and whatnot. Oh it was a Mess, Papa said, but they wadn't no sign a'my Brother Herman no wheres so I had Hope he wadn't Dead but only just run off some wheres to hide from who ever it was a'trying to do him Harm. But then, Papa said, I looked out the Back Door and I seen some-body's Foot a'Sticking up out a'Old Karl's Burn Pile. I knowed just who's it was too. Oh Herman, I said, Oh Herman Oh Herman Oh Herman. Calley and Annie come over to hold me cause I was already a'Crying and Calley said Who you think Murdered your Brother Herman and I said, Big Nose and Lit-tle Ears them two Dead Men who killed each other that night. They told me they Murdered Sheriff Highschoote and the Judge and some o'Farm Boy. I reckon my Brother Herman is that o'Farm Boy they was talking bout huh. Probably wanted his Money, Calley said, then Killed him when he wouldn't tell em where he had it hid. I reckon so, Papa said, o'Herman wouldn't a'just give it over to em. No Sir, Calley said, the o'Greedy Herman I knowed a'give up his own Life fore he'd a'give up his Money.

It took some doing, Papa said, but we got my Brother Herman up out a'Old Karl's Burn Pile then wrapped him up in a Blanket and rode him on back to the Choats and Mister and Miz Choat was Glad to have him there in they Grave Yard long with ever body else cause o'Herman was still Family even if he was Hard to get long with most a'the time and didn't much care bout no body but his own self.

AFTER WE WAS DONE WITH COVERING HERMAN UP and drying our Eyes, Papa said, I asked Marcellus if he wanted to come Long with me and Calley and catch Wild Horses out the Brush to sell and trade to Make our Living from but he said No his Job was taking care a'little Bird now so o'Jeffey could talk out his mouth when some body needed to hear some thing from the Other Side. And theys always some body needs that, he said. Wonder if theys some body over there knows for sure it was them two Dead Men Murdered my Brother Herman and Sheriff Highschoot and the Judge I said. They's probably some body knows for sure, Marcellus said, but that don't mean they gonna tell you. Well why wouldn't they tell me, Papa said, I don't see Why Not. I don't know, Marcellus said. They just got Rules I reckon and some times theys Things they won't tell no body cause ever body got to Live they own Life as it comes and not take no Short Cuts or they might have to come back and Live it all over again. Who says so, Papa said. I think ever body says so for they own self, Marcellus said, but I don't know Nothing bout it for sure just maybe one or two things Granny Jeffey tole me is all. Like what, Papa said. Like you ain't no Smarter over theren you are here, Marcellus said, but you got all the Time in the World to work on it over there and they's all kinds a'People gonna help you if you let em. O'Jeffey says all you gotta do is Ask, he said, and they come a'Running but you gotta be careful who you get cause some of em don't even know they Dead yet and wanna take a Ride on you specially if you a Drinker and a Smoker cause they liked it so much they self when they was a'Live and still want some more of it even if they Dead now. Well I don't Drink or Smoke neither one, Papa said, so I don't reckon I got to worry bout Some Body a'wanting to take a'Ride on me. O'Jeffey says it's the same thing bout wanting the Womens as it is with wanting the Drinking and the Smoking, Marcellus said, but she wouldn't splain it to me.

*M*IZ CHOAT DIDN'T WANT ANNIE TO GO WITH US, Papa said, and said No you stay here with us Annie you ain't got no Business out there in the Brush while these two go off a'Chasing Wild Horses. Why I'm gonna be right there with em, Annie said. You don't think I'm just gonna go set by the Fire do you. Well I would, Miz Choat said. I don't believe that for a minute Miz Choat, Annie said. No Ma'am not for a Minute. I just wouldn't want nothing to happen to you Annie is all, Miz Choat said. Thank You Miz Choat, Annie said, I wouldn't want nothing to happen to you neither. Oh and then, Papa said, Mister and Miz Choat give us some Chickens and two Pigs to get our new Life started on and some Hugs for ever body specially one for Annie like she was they own Daughter and we went a'riding off back to the Old Home Place o'Johnny riding with Annie and me and o'Calley a'leading the way with Possum and Fritz and that poor Little o'One Eyed Bear a'walking long side. Where's that Brush you said was full a'Wild Horses, Calley said. All up and down the Blanco River like I said, Papa said. We just got to go Look for em is all. No ain't no body going any wheres til we get settled in our new Home Annie said. Well I'll say this for us, o'Calley said, we ain't lacking a Boss out here in the Wilderness are we and then, Papa said, Johnny bout fell off the Horse a'Laughing bout it til Annie tole him he was just gonna have to Walk on his own two Feet if he was gonna act like that and he dried it right up. This is a Adventure we a'going on here ain't it, Annie said, and Papa said Yes it is I'm just sorry my Brother Herman ain't long with us on it. May be we'll name the First Wild Horse we catch Herman after him, Calley said, If that makes you feel better. Yes Sir it would, Papa said, and Him too I reckon. Maybe we'll name a Horse after each and ever one a'the People we Loved but who already gone on, Annie said, but Calley said No he didn't think that was a Good Idea cause we wouldn't never wanna Sell em or Trade em a'way then and that's the quickest way they is to go out the Horse Busness when you just Starting. And then Johnny went to Laughing bout that too but Annie just let it go this time cause she thought it was Funny too, Papa said.

*T*HEY WAS STILL SOME OATS in the Barn for the Horses, Papa said, and Annie cooked one a'the Chickens for our Suppers then set o'Johnny at the Head a'the Table like he was Genral Houston at a Party and you never seen no body Happyier in all you Whole Life. Now he's gonna wanna set there like that ever time Calley said. You don't know what you done Young Lady. Bout time he's getting treated like a Regular Person, Annie said, It don't hurt nothing. Then, Papa said, she give o'Johnny a little Knock on his Head and said Does it Johnny but Johnny didn't have no Idea what she was talkng bout and just set there like a Knot on a Log. You gonna help us catch Wild Horses Johnny, Calley said, we gonna need all the Help we can get and that goes for you Rowdy Boys too he said and pointed his Finger at Fritz and o'Possum and that Little Bear but, Papa said, they didn't have no more Idea what he was talking bout then o'Johnny did. They gonna have to take Lessons on catching Wild Horses,

Annie said, and me too I reckon. They ain't much to it, Papa said. You just scatter some Oats over there by a Water Hole and when the Wild Horses come up to eat em a'bite you just jump out from your Hiding Place and rope a'couple of em. Then Hang On, he said, that's how me and Old Karl used to do it. That's pretty much like how you catch a Poler Bear too ain't it, Calley said. You ain't never caught a Poler Bear have you Mister Pearsall Annie said. No Ma'am, Calley said, but I know a Man used to catch em and he told me How. How, Annie said. Well first you cut a Big Hole in the Ice, Calley said, and scatter some Green Peas all round it Then when the o'Poler Bear comes up to take a Pea you Kick him in the Ice Hole. Then o'Calley bout fell down on the Floor a'Laughing at his own Joke like he always did.

I GIVE ANNIE ME AND MY BROTHER'S OLD ROOM

to sleep in and went out on the Front Porch to sleep with the Dogs and Johnny and Calley and that Little o'One Eyed Bear, Papa said, and then here come Annie out on the Porch with her Blanket to sleep by me. Annie you better get on back in the House fore some body sees you I said and she said I just wanna be by you We aint a'gonna do nothing are we. Not that I know of, Papa said. May be some day she said, Papa said, and give me a little Smile to go with it. You already seen me Neckid any how, Annie said, Remember. Yes I do remember Annie I said, but I didn't mean to That was just a accident when I pulled that curtain back. I been thinking you oughta show me you self Neckid one a'these days just to make us even, she said. No I ain't gonna do that Annie, Papa said, I like it just fine how I am with my Clothes on. Well you can't stay that way with your Clothes on all you Life, she said. I'm gonna catch you Neckid one a'these Days same way you done me. Well you might and you might not, Papa said, let's just go to Sleep now We got Wild Horses to go catch Tomorra. Okay Annie said then scooched up right against me and give me bout ten squeezes. Annie I said, Papa said, I don't believe I can go to sleep with you a'doing that. Why not Annie said, Don't this make you feel Safe me a'holding on to you like this. It does me she said. Okay, Papa said, just hold on any way you want to and I won't say nothing more bout it. So, he said, in a minute we was sound a'sleep and only thing you could hear was o'Johnny and that Little o'One Eyed Bear over there just a'Snoring and ever once in a'while o'Fritz a'going Heh Heh Heh in his Dream but then, Papa said, I felt this Hand come up and run down my Face and I thought it was Annie a'doing it but then of a sudden it come to me No that Hand was coming from in front a'me some wheres and not from in back behind me where Annie was and I opened my Eye to see who it was and Why it was my Momma just a'Shimmering and a'Smiling at me and a'Standing there with her was this other Lady bout Momma's size and she was a'Petting Annie's Face and even if I never seen this Lady fore in all my Life I knowed xactly who she was and Who she was, Papa said, was Annie's Momma and her and my Momma was both here to see how we was a'doing and was we Alright. And Oh, Papa said, then I really did feel Safe and went on back to Sleep.

*N*EXT MORNING BRIGHT AND EARLY, Papa said, a'way we went with our Bucket a'Oats down to the Creek to catch us some Wild Horses if we could and on the Way Calley said Ever Body be just quiet as Little Mice a'going through here and we pretty much was and then he said we set back in our Hiding Place to wait with our Ropes ready to Rope them Horses with when they come to eat the Oats but No, Papa said, didn't no Horses come but only Deers and Possums and Coons and a Hava-lina Hog and a'couple a'other critters we couldn't see in the Dark til Calley throwed a'little Rock and scared em off. Oh we set there and we set there and we set there, Papa said, then Calley said Wheres all them Wild Horses you been a'Talking bout. You sure this is the Right Place where you and your mean o'Daddy used to catch em. May be they still Sleeping, Papa said, its early yet and Annie said I'm gonna go back to Sleep my self if some thing don't come a'long here pretty quick then reached over and give o'Fritz a push to quit Licking on his Hiney. Why they do that she said Seems like ever Dog I ever knowed in my Life does that. Don't nobody know Why, o'Calley said, it's one a'the Great Mysteries a'the World like them Big Pearmids over there where ever they are. Egip, Annie said, Ain't that Right. Egip, Calley said, Yes Ma'am that is Right I just forgot. Then of a sudden, Papa said, Johnny come a'Live and seen some thing didn't none a'the rest a'us see and that was a'big o'White Some Thing or Other a'coming out the Brush to the Water Hole and so, Papa said, we all just set there not even a'Breathing to see what it was but it stayed just out a'sight to where you couldn't tell Who or What it was. What is that, Annie said, I never seen the Like. Me neither, Papa said, It looks like a Ghost a'some kind or Other don't it. Might be some o'Pioneer in his Covered Wagon got Lost some wheres long the way, Calley said, but I'm just guessing cause I don't have no more Idea bout it'n yall do. Oh and then, Papa said, why o'Johnny of a sudden got up on his Feet and went a'crawling out there in the Brush to see what it was his self and we all Hollered No Johnny NO cause we was scared for him but he didn't pay us no mine and went on til we couldn't even see him no more out there in the Brush some wheres.

*O*H WE DIDN'T KNOW WHAT TO DO, Papa said, and then we heared all this Snorting and Snuffling sounded like some body's Pants was on Fire back there in the Brush and I bout jumped and run to save o'Johnny if I could, he said, but Calley grabbed me by my Shirt and pulled me back. It's Okay, he said. They just Talking is all. Who's just Talking I said, Papa said, and Calley said o'Johnny and that Ghost Horse they just Talking things over. So we just set down there to wait and I said How you know they just Talking and Calley said cause I can hear em Talking and I know they ain't nothing to Worry bout. Well what're they Talking bout then, Papa said. I don't know, Calley said, they just getting to know one a'nother is all I reckon. See if they gonna be Friends or not. And then I listened, Papa said and they wadn't Snorting and Snuffling no more like they was before. I don't hear nothing no more I said and Annie said No I don't hear nothing neither and then Calley said Well I reckon o'Johnny and that Ghost Horse is a'getting long just Fine then huh. So we just set there some more and wadn't long fore o'Possum and that Little o'One Eyed Bear went on back to sleep there on the ground and Fritz started a'Licking on his Hiney again like always but Annie said Stop it Stop it right now Fritz and he did Stop it but he give her a Look to say Why don't you just let me a'lone bout it Lady. And then of a sudden we heared the Brush a'Rattling a'gain and after bout two years here come o'Johnny out the Brush then after a'nother two three years why here come this Beautiful White Stallion looked like some Horse broke a'loose out a'Pretty Pitchur some wheres and then, Papa said, after a'nother minute or two here come a little Momma Horse a'follering long behind and behind that Momma Horse was a'little Baby Horse but Oh, he said, they wadn't from out the same Pitchur that Ghost Horse was cause they was both so Bloody and Beat Up to where it Broke your Heart just to see em.

OH THAT POOR MOMMA AND HER LITTLE BABY, Annie said, some body been a'Beating on em and Oh it was True Papa said. Why they was Bloody Beat Marks all up and down em both and the Momma had a'Bloody Face where some body hit her may be three four times with a Chain. Let's get em to the Barn, Calley said, we can't do nothing for em here so Johnny went a'Limping back to the Barn best he could and them Hurt Horses just follered long behind like little Sheep and so did the rest a'us. Who'd do such a Mean Thing to a Creature Annie said and Papa said, Why my mean o'Daddy would a'done such a thing when he was a'Live I seen him do it my self. Then Annie reached out her Hand and give one of em a nice Pet and said Well ain't no body ever gonna Beat em again and then I looked round, Papa said, and I seen Calley and Johnny and Fritz and o'Possum and that Little o'One Eyed Bear and Sister and Firefoot and Annie's Horse Diamond was all a'greeing with Her on that too. They need Doctoring Calley said So, Papa said, me and him and Annie went up to the House to get some Bee Honey and mix up some Snow Liniment for they Cuts and Bruises and Hit Marks and while we was in there, Calley said They's a mean Son of a Bitch a'Loose out there in the Country some wheres a'Hurting Little Horses and when I catch him he's god dam sure gonna know it Mister. I been a'Living round here all my Life, Papa said, and I never seen no body beat a Horse like these two here been Beat cept my own Daddy. Well they's some body else out there a'beating Horses now ain't they, Annie said, may be even two three of em. Well we gonna see bout that fore we done with it, Calley said and I could tell he meant ever Word a'what he said, Papa said. Then we went on back down there in the Barn and when we got in there we seen Fritz and o'Possum and that Little o'One Eyed Bear was all being Nice to that Hurt Momma and her Little Baby but that Big White Ghost Horse was gone now. And not only him, Papa said, but o'Johnny was gone long with him.

And then of a sudden we heared the Brush
a'Rattling a'gain and after bout two years
here come o'Johnny out the Brush . . .

*T*HEN NEXT THING,
Papa said, was that little Baby Horse of a sudden took him a'couple a'steps
and went down to the ground and couldn't get up no more. Oh and then,
he said, why his Momma started Crying and went over there and tried to
push her Little Boy back up on his Feet with her Nose but No it didn't work
and he just layed there and then, he said, Me and Annie and Calley all three
a'us got down on our Knees and lifted that poor Baby up on his Feet a'gain
and Oh his Momma just went to Kissing on him and Crying bout it she was
so Happy but No when we took our Hands out from under him why he just
dropped back down to where we lifted him up from in the First Place. No
No No Sweetie, Annie said, you got to get up and Walk. Then, Papa said,
Annie got down there on her Knees again and started lifting with all her
might but she couldn't do no Good so me and Calley give her a Hand and in
a Minute we had that little Booger back up on his Feet and started Walking
him a'round and a'round so he'd get the Idear and remember how to do it on
his own but No ever time we let go a'him why he'd stagger round like some
o'Drunk Man and fall back down a'gain. And Oh, Papa said, his Momma
Cried and Cried bout it and so did Fritz and o'Possum and that Little o'One
Eyed Bear. And me and Annie and o'Calley too, he said, So we tryed it a'gain
and a'gain and a'gain and his poor o'Momma'd foller us a'round just a'Crying
ever step a'the way and a'shaking her head No No No Oh Please No No No
No but that didn't do the Job neither and that Little Baby Horse went down
a'gain His Eyes just a'Rolling all round like he was trying to get him one Last
Look at the World fore it was too Late and then, Papa said, I got down there
with him and whispered in his Ear Don't Go Don't Go It's gonna Break your
o'Momma's Heart if you Go and then, he said, I seen this little Spark a'Light
way down there in side his Eye like a Lightning Bug and Oh it went to flying Down Down Down like it was Looking for some other World way Down
there Deeper'n this one here. Oh and then, Papa said, that Little Lightning
Bug in side his Eye went to Shimmering like it was bout to go out but No,
he said, now here come a'Bunch more Lightning Bugs up from out the Dark
just a'Flickering OnOff OnOff OnOff like that and they went over there and
grabbed on to that First Lightning Bug in side his Eye and now they was just
one Big Bright Lightning Bug a'Blinking OnOff OnOff OnOff like they was
the Heart Beat a'the Whole World. Oh and then, Papa said, they give out
one Last Big Flash a'Light and then they was Gone. And then Firefoot and

Sister and Annie's Horse Diamond and that poor o'Momma Horse all went to Crying long with the Creatures and ever body else. That Little Baby's Gone now ain't he Annie said and I said Yes he is Annie. Gone Gone Gone.

W E BURIED THAT LITTLE BABY HORSE, Papa said, then Calley said One a'us got to stay here and take care a'this Momma Horse, and the other two gotta go find Johnny and that Ghost Horse. I'll stay, Annie said, I know that's what yall was gonna say any how. We'll be back Annie, Papa said, won't be long. It's okay, Annie said, I wouldn't a'run off and left this Momma all by her self even if yall'd a'tole me to. I ain't known you all that long in my Life, Calley said, but I already knowed they ain't no body can tell you much a'any thing any how. Then he Smiled at her and me and him and the Creatures rode on out a'there with a Smile but then our Smile dried up, Papa said, cause we couldn't find no Tracks to foller. This don't make no sense, Calley said. Ever thing that steps on the Earth leaves a Track don't it. That's what I always heared, Papa said, and I never seen no different. Hey you Critters he hollered at Fritz and o'Possum and that Little o'One Eyed Bear, Go Find us some Tracks to Foller cause we coming up Short here. Oh and then, Papa said, Why all three of em went to Running round and a'Sniffing ever wheres but No they didn't come up with no moren we did. Maybe they sprouted Wings and took off a'Flying, Calley said. You ever think bout that. No Sir, Papa said, but I'd like to see it if they did. So we rode that Country round all day long and didn't see no Sign a'o'Johnny or that Ghost Horse neither one. Then Long bout Dark, Papa said, I said Calley you know I'm starting to get a'little Worried bout them two ain't you and o'Calley said I wadn't never gonna even mention it but Yes Sir I am getting a little Worried my Self. So we made us a big Circle over by the Blanco River just to be sure they wadn't there and lit for Home with the Creatures and we could see they was Worried too bout much as we was. This been a Surprise to me, Calley said, I a'never thought o'Johnny'd run off like that in the First Place. You don't figgur some thing Bad just jumped up and got em both do you Calley, Papa said. I don't know what to figgur, Calley said. I just never seen nothing like it in all my Life is all, he said.

83

BUT WHEN WE WENT BACK IN THE BARN, Papa said, Why there was o'Johnny and that Ghost Horse a'eating some Oats and they had a'nother Horse with em and some o'Mule had his foot all tore up from when some body hobbled him with a piece a'Bob Wire but Annie was already a'Doctoring it. They brung us two more needs Doctoring, she said, What's a'going on here. I don't know, Calley said. No Sir I don't know neither I said, Papa said, It's like we running a'Doctor House for Horses here ain't it, Annie said, but I'm Glad to do it. Well we all Glad to do it Annie, Calley said and give that o'Mule some more Oats out his hand, but I don't know how we gonna start a Horse Busness with a'Bunch a'cripply Horses like we got here do you he said. They gonna get better, Annie said, They ain't nothing to Worry bout. Only thing I'm Worried bout, Calley said, is what we gonna do oncet they eat up all the Oats we got in here and got to go out-side and eat Grass like ever other Horse ever borned in the World. I don't see nothing Wrong with that, Annie said. Here's what's Wrong with that, Calley said, Some body might come a'riding a'long by here and See em and they ain't even ours for Some body to see. You think they might think we stole em huh, Papa said. Is that what you a'Thinking. I'm a'Thinking they's a bunch a'things we didn't never do, Calley said, but they a'wanting to Hang us for em any how and I don't see no reason to add to they List if we can help it. I agree with ever thing you say, Annie said. We'll just keep a'Doctoring on em in the Barn til we run out a'Oats then put em to eating Grass some wheres where can't no body see em ain't that Right. Yes Ma'am I believe that is xactly Right Calley said and I said Yes Ma'am I do too, Papa said, but o'Johnny was over there a'petting the Horses like they was his Little Chilren and didn't pay us no mine. You know what, Calley said, I think o'Johnny is starting to think he's a'Horse his self. And, Papa said, I was starting to think the same thing my self.

NEXT MORNING, Papa said, wadn't only o'Johnny and the Big White Ghost Horse was gone but now so was o'Firefoot too and Calley bout had a Fit bout it. Firefoot never done some thing like this in his whole Life, he said, What in the god dam Hell's going on here. But me and Annie didn't have no Idea what was a'going on here neither, Papa said, then Calley said Could he borrow Sister and go a'Looking for Firefoot his self but Sister was over there a'Nuzzling that o'Mule and wouldn't go. Well have you own dam way bout it, Calley said, I'll go on my own two Feet then less they gone Sassy on me too. Well I'm a'going with you I said, Papa said, they's some thing Funny going on here if you ask me. And it's getting Funnier all the time, Annie said, but ain't none a'us a'Laughing bout it are we.

So me and Calley and the Creatures took off a'walking cross the Country to see if we couldn't find where o'Johnny and the Big White Horse and now o'Firefoot all gone off to and Oh we Walked and we Walked and we Walked some more til we was bout wore out from it cause we was ordinarily Horse Back Riders and not Foot Walkers like now. Then of a sudden, Papa said, we heared this Horse a'Screaming way off out yonder some wheres and we Run to go see what was a'going on and then we come on Top a'this little Hill and Oh now we seen some o'Farmer way off down there in his Corn Field a'Beating his o'Plow Horse with a Stick to make him go and that poor o'Plow Horse was just a'Jumping and a'Crying bout it and course, Papa said, o'Calley pulled his big o'Pistola out his Pants cause wadn't no body gonna treat a Horse that way long as he had some thing to say bout it. But, Papa said, bout that time we seen some thing start to kicking up a big Puff a'Dust that come a'rolling cross that Farmer's Corn Field right at him like a Whirled Wind Storm and then it stopped and out jumped that Big White Ghost Horse and o'Firefoot and Johnny too and wadn't but a second and them two Horses went to Screaming and Kicking and Biting at that Mean o'Farmer and sent him a'Running off cross his Corn Field like his Pants was on Fire and while they was a'doing that, Papa said, why o'Johnny was over there a'setting that o'Plow Horse Free to run off with the big White Horse and Firefoot.

O'JOHNNY AND FIREFOOT IS HORSE THEIFS,

Calley said, you know it Mister. Yes Sir I just seen it with my own two Eyes, Papa said, or I wouldn't a'never Believed it my self. It's that big White Horse a'putting em up to it, Calley said. He's just trying to Help Horses that needs Help the way I see it, Papa said. I won't say nothing Bad bout him for it.

85

Here's some thing Bad bout it, Calley said, it makes us Horse Theifs too same as them and when they go to Hanging some body for it It ain't gonna just be a couple a'Horses. You know that Devil's Fork we been talking bout he said. Yes Sir, Papa said. Well we on it now for sure ain't we, Calley said, and we got two Choices we can make. On the one Hand, he said, we can run that Big White Horse off and tell o'Johnny to quit a'doing what he's been a'doing but then all them Horses out there in the World gonna still just keep on getting Mistreated but that ain't a Choice neither cause ain't neither one a'us ever gonna permit that are we Amigo. No Sir not me, Papa said. No Sir. So what it comes down to is this, Calley said, We just gonna have to go long with it See Where it takes us. Which Fork is it we a'taking then, Papa said. I don't reckon we gonna know which one we a'taking til we get to the End of it and see, Calley said, but by then it might be too god dam late to ever turn back.

SO WE WALKED ON BACK TO THE HOUSE, Papa said, and tole Annie bout o'Johnny and Firefoot and that Big White Horse all going round Stealing Horses to keep em from being mistreated all the time and she almost Cryed she was so Happy they'd do such a'Nice thing. But here's the Bad Part, Calley said, that o'Farmer seen em and if he sees em a'gain he's gonna wanna know where in the Hell is my Plow Horse that yall run off with and then he's gonna go to Looking all over the Country for it and probably come a'Riding by here one day while he's at it. Oh and it was just bout then, Papa said, Why here come o'Johnny and Firefoot and that Big White Horse in the Barn with that o'Plow Horse we was a'talking bout and Annie said Let's go on and Doctor him then find us a Secret Place to hide all these Horses at cause I got a Feeling they's gonna be a'lot more a'Coming ever time you turn your Head and Look Round. Then, Papa said, I remembered this Place called The Narrows that wadn't nothing but a big giant Crack in the Ground where the Blanco River come a'Running through after a'falling off this big Cliff at the top and they's Grass Grass Grass all at the Bottom for how many ever Horses you got. I heared a'that Place, Calley said, but I never seen it. I never even Heared of it, Annie said, but course I ain't from round here neither. So, Papa said, we Doctored that o'Plow Horse best we could and next Morning went over to The Narrows and found a slanty Trail down to the bottom and Oh it was so Pretty why you'd a thought you was in Heaven some wheres what with all the Vines and Flowers and what-not a'growing there. Then, he said, Annie hollered Yall come look a'here at this and we went over there and Oh they was this big Room back behind the Water Fall where you could hide least a'hunderd or two Horses and couldn't no body see Nothing even if they was a'Looking for em.

THEN, Papa said, we went back to the House and got all the Bee Honey and Snow Liniment and even a Needle and some Thread to sew up Cuts if we had to and brung all the Mistreated Horses back to they new Home down there in The Narrows. I wouldn't mine living here my self, Calley said, cept for all these Horses ever where and Oh, Papa said, we got a Laugh out a'that and so did o'Fritz with a little Heh Heh Heh of his own. They Happy here, Annie said, I never seen no Horses Happier in my Life have you. And I said, Papa said, No I ain't never neither. Well, Calley said, we wanted to get in the Horse Busness and now by god we in it ain't we. Course we gonna have to sell one or two fore we can really say we in the Horse Busness. But not never to no Mean People, Annie said. No Sir not never to no Mean People. I give her a Nod, Papa said, cause I was the same way bout it my self and course so was o'Calley. But this is gonna be a Tricky Deal here, he said, cause these is all Stolen Horses and one or two of em even got a'Brand on em that says so. They gonna Hang us if they catch us trying to sell Stolen Horses ain't they, Papa said. Ain't that the way it works. It is, Calley said, then Annie said Well then we'll just give em a'way to Nice People. Oh and then a Idea come to me, Papa said, and I said Or just turn em a'loose when they all Healed up and let em go start a new Life where evers else they want to. O'Johnny was over there a'Petting on the Horses when I said that, Papa said, but he heared what I said and liked it so much he went to Grinning and Nodding like some o'Loonie and Annie said It wouldn't surprise me one bit if o'Johnny went over there and lived with em too you know it. Yes Sir and they'd be Glad to have him, Calley said, don't you reckon. And then, Papa said, I looked over there and all them Stolen Horses was pushing and shoving on each other to get close nough to o'Johnny to where he could give em a'Pet on they Head or a'Scratch on they Ear. And then, he said, I looked the other way and I seen o'Calley a'setting over there all by his self a'twirling his Spur Ching e Ching e ChingChingChing and I knowed he was a'Wishing Pela Rosa was here with him. Either that, Papa said, or he was a'Wishing he was over there on the Shimmery Side with her.

O UR HORSE THEIFS went out ever day, Papa said, and they always come back in a Day or Two with some more Horses been Mistreated by some body or other and needed Doctoring and me and Annie was always ready to go with the Bee Honey and the Snow Liniment less we was out and had to go up to the Barn and make us some more. One day we was up there in the Barn a'doing that, he said, when some body rode up out side and hollered Hello the Barn Hello the Barn and I seen it was that o'Farmer mistreated his Plow Horse out there in his Corn Field that Day. Yes Sir I said, Papa said, who you a'looking for Mister and he said No I ain't looking for no body I'm a'looking for my o'Plow Horse some body run off with the other Day. You know who it was run off with it, Annie said, may be we seen em some wheres. Well two of em was Horses they self, the Farmer said, and the other one looked like a'little o'German Sausage only had little short arms bout this long on him, he said, then made believe he was cutting his own arms off bout at the elbow. No we ain't never seen no body looked like that, Papa said. Course we ain't been Looking for some body looked like that neither. What bout these other two Horses you talking bout here, Annie said. You get a good look at em. Big strong Horses both of em, the Farmer said, one of em White as the Hair on you o'Granma's Head. I Seen a'big Black One the other Day, Papa said, but No not no White One. No me neither, Annie said, and I didn't see that big Black One neither like he did. Yall don't find that peculiar the o'Farmer said, them Horses stealing a'nother Horse like that. I didn't know what to say, Papa said, and Annie didn't neither so we just stood there a'Looking at him and didn't say nothing and then here in a minute or so he give us a Funny Look and went a'riding round the Back a'the Barn to see what all was back there then went on off the same way he come from in the First Place.

WHEN WE GOT BACK TO THE NARROWS, Papa said, Why there was Sister a'trying to help Johnny up on the Big White Horse by Sticking her nose tween his Legs and giving him a Lift Up. They been a'trying to teach o'Johnny how to ride a Horse, Calley said, but it ain't Easy cause his Arms and Fingers is too short to hang on with. Oh and then of a sudden, Papa said, Sister give Johnny a Lift so big it bout throwed him off on the other side but No Johnny stayed up on the White Horse's back then just set there like Genral Houston on o'Whats His Name and went to Grinning. Now the Trick's gonna be keeping him up there so he don't fall off in the Cactuses some wheres. They's some thing else we got to tell you bout o'Johnny, Papa said. That Farmer seen him when they stole his o'Plow Horse the other Day so he knows what he looks like if he ever sees him a'gain. How you know this Calley said and Annie said Cause he come a'looking for his o'Plow Horse up at the Barn when we was there and tole us. Oh this ain't Good, Calley said, No Sir this ain't Good at all some body seen Johnny helping steal a Plow Horse off some o'Farmer. Well we just gonna have to hide him so don't nobody never see him again, Papa said, that's all aint it but then we looked round and there went o'Johnny a'riding off on that Big White Horse and just a'flapping his little Arms like a Bird he liked it so much. Oncet you put a Man a'Horse Back in the World, Calley said, you ain't a'never gonna get him back a'Foot again and I give you my Word on that he said. Oh and it was True, Papa said, Why you couldn't a'pulled o'Johnny off that big White Horse with two Mules and a Chain after that. He wouldn't even get off to Eat his Suppers neither and Annie had to reach it up to him from the Ground like he was the King a'Spain or some where but Oh, Papa said, he sure did learn to ride that Big White Horse and it wadn't but bout two three Days and they was a'Running and a'Jumping over Cactuses and whatnot ever wheres you looked and no Trouble a'doing it at all. They become like one Animal tween em, Papa said, one Part that Big White Ghost Horse and the other Part o'Johnny his self And, he said, you couldn't hardly tell where one Part ended and the other Part started cause they was so much just the One together.

WADN'T LONG AFTER THAT,

Papa said, and we had two Gangs a'Horse Theifs a'going Out ever Day to steal Mistreated Horses and other Creatures been mistreated too when they run a'cross em like a Goat and one Day a Mexkin Donkey. The Big White Horse with o'Johnny on top was the Boss a'one Bunch and Firefoot and some time Sister too was the Boss a'the other Bunch and Oh me and Annie couldn't believe how many Mistreated Horses they was out there in the Country and we put our Hand to Doctoring em ever one and give em a Good Home there in The Narrows til they was well a'gain and could go off some wheres on they own if they wanted to but No they never did. But one Day, Papa said, they was this little Paint Horse come in with all the other Stolen Horses and he had a Bullet Hole in his Leg where some body Shot him with a Gun and Calley said Oh this is Bad Bad Bad. Now they gone to Shooting at our Horse Theifs to keep em from a'stealing theirs ain't they. And I reckon they hit one a'they own by chance he said. Annie was already over there a'Doctoring on it, Papa said, and said He's lucky it didn't hit no Bone. I'd rather have Luck moren bout any thing else in the World, Calley said, but you can't always count on it a'being there when you need it the most can you. I believe that too Mister Pearsall, Annie said, but I don't have no Idea what you trying to say here. I'm saying I'm scared for our Horses and getting more scared for em ever day what with People a'Shooting at em now like they was regular Horse Theifs. You gonna tell our Horses to just quit Stealing other Horses from here on out, Papa said. They wouldn't pay no attention to me even if I did, Calley said. Our Horses see a Wrong and they just gonna try to Fix it Right a'gain even if some body Shoots em Dead for it. Oh that give me and Annie a'feeling a'Cold Ice a'Running Up and Down our Backs, Papa said, but we didn't know what to do bout it. What we gonna do bout it then I said, Papa said and Calley didn't say Nothing for a long time but then he looked over at Fritz and o'Possum and that Little o'One Eyed Bear and he said I think what we need is some Guards to warn em when some body's a'Coming so they can get the Hell outta there fore its too late. And I reckon we got three pretty good ones right here don't we, he said.

$\mathcal{S}$o,

Papa said, we sent Fritz and o'Possum and that Little o'One Eyed Bear out a'head a'the Big White Horse and Johnny and they Gang a'Horse Theifs the next Morning so they could see if they was any body a'waiting for em in the Bushes some wheres to Shoot em when they come to steal Mistreated Horses but first two three days No they couldn't find no Horses been Mistreated any wheres and Annie said may be the People round here decided to be Good to they Horses from now on out. But, Papa said, on the fourth day we come up on this Man a'beating his Horse in the Pen out there behind his Barn and Oh that poor Horse was just a'Screaming and a'Crying from it and you couldn't hardly hold o'Johnny and the Big White Horse and them Others back they was so bent on Stealing that Horse fore he got Beat some more. And they would a'tried it too, Papa said, cept of a sudden o'Possum and Fritz and that Little o'One Eyed Bear smelled some thing Bad a'coming out from the Barn and they run down there just a'Howling and a'Growling and run on in the Barn and then they was some more Hollering but this time it come from inside the Barn and then Oh here come three Men with Big Guns a'Running out the Barn where they been a'hiding with o'Possum and Fritz and that Little o'One Eyed Bear on they Tail and they run on off fast as they could and so did that other Fella who been a'Beating his Horse in the Pen and when he did, Papa said, why o'Johnny give the Big White Horse his Heel then run on down there and Jumped the Fence like they wadn't nothing to it then come on back up to us with that Mistreated Horse a'limping long behind best he could. I don't like how this is working out, Calley said. They setting Traps to catch us and they Mistreating Horses for they Bait.

$\mathcal{L}$ATE THAT EVENING,

Papa said, me and Annie and o'Fritz went up to the House to get us a'Chicken for our Suppers and there was Marcellus and Bird a'setting out on the Porch waiting for us. Yall always a Surprise a'one kind or a'nother ain't you I said and Marcellus said o'Jeffey piped up here a'while a'go and said she got some thing she wants to tell yall. What is it, Papa said, we always glad to get a Word or Two from o'Jeffey. Oh and then Marcellus set Bird down on my Knee and

Bird looked up at me and opened his mouth and out come o'Jeffey's voice. Yall doing a Good Thing for all them Mistreated Horses yall been a'Stealing, she said, but don't Ever Body in the World like it. Yes Ma'am, Annie said, we know that. Yes Ma'am we do, Papa said. But here's some thing else yall may be don't know, o'Jeffey said, It ain't only yall a'Stealing them Mistreated Horses they don't like. What they don't like even moren that is yall acting like some o'Scrawny Horse out there in the Pasture is just important as Some Human Being a'setting in his House. Well I reckon that's just how we see it Miz Jeffey, Papa said. We don't mean nothing by it. Well some People don't like it worth a Lick, she said, cause they fraid What if its True. Well it is True, Annie said, ain't it. Yes Ma'am from over here a Animal just important as some o'Man, she said, but from where yall at it ain't always so. Some People think they Rising Up ever time they beat some poor Critter Down but the Fact is, o'Jeffey said, Can't no body Rise Up til ever Ever Body all Rise Up together cause we all just in One Big Boat and they ain't nothing to do bout it cept Paddle a'long together so don't No Body sink. Where'd that Big White Horse come from any how, Papa said. I never seen nothing like this til he come a'long. Oh, o'Jeffey said, they's always some Big White Horse round but what you got to remember, she said, is they always some Big Black Horse come round too at the same time cause you don't never just get the One with out you get the Other. Why's that Miss Jeffey, Annie said, and o'Jeffey said cause Ever Thing just always travel in Pairs Hon. The White One don't never mean nothing less you got the Black One to make you see it. Like Up don't mean nothing without you got a Down. Same thing with Wet and Dry or Here and There or Yes and No or Him and Her or, she said, Good and Bad.

*T*HEN A FUNNY THING

started happening, Papa said. Horses that hadn't never even been Mistreated started a'coming in at The Narrows. Oh they come in Twos and Threes and Sevens and Eights and some times in Tens and Twelves and, he said, they come from all Directions too North South East West even from over yonder near where Kendalia is and the Mommas and the Daddys and they Little Babies they all come in a Big Bunch. They gonna Eat Us out a'House

Then a funny thing started happening, Papa said
Horses that hadn't never even been Mistreated
started a'coming in at The Narrows

and Home too ain't they, o'Calley said, but he was just Joking cause ever Day them Horses'd go out on they own and find they own Grass to eat. Then First Thing they'd do when they got back in The Narrows, Papa said, was crowd a'round o'Johnny and that big White Horse like they was King One and King Two a'the World and o'Johnny'd lean down off the Big White Horse and Jabber at em bout some thing or other in Horse Talk and they Ears would perk up and they Head would just go to nodding like they under stood ever Word he said. What you figgur o'Johnny's saying to em, Annie said and Calley come right back at her and said Sorry I don't speak nough Horse Talk to know Annie and Oh, Papa said, we got us a big Laugh out a'that. But, he said, I think o'Fritz and Possum and that Little o'One Eyed Bear could talk Horse Talk cause I'd look over there and all three of em'd be up on that Big White Horse with Johnny and o'Johnny'd be jabbering some thing at a Horse and o'Fritz'd go Heh Heh Heh and o'Possum'd go to Howl-ing like it was bout the Funniest thing he ever did hear his self and so would that Little o'One Eyed Bear and I couldn't hardly Help my self neither, Papa said, and I'd just go to Laughing right long with em even if I didn't have no idea what the Joke was. What're you Laughing bout Mister, Annie said, and I said No I don't have no Idea What bout and then Oh we both went to Laughing bout that too.

*T*HEN THEM NEW HORSES went to going out with them other Horses ever Morning to save all the Mis-treated Horses they could find, Papa said, and wadn't long fore they wadn't hardly no more Mistreated Horses in our part a'the Country to find and they had to go down there toward San Antoneya to find some more and bring em on back to The Narrows. Oh and Them was bout the Happiest Horses you ever did see in your Life, he said, even if some of em been so Bad Mistreated they couldn't hardly get round on they own four Feet. This is like a Secret Horse Town we got here ain't it, Annie said. Ain't nothing down here but Horses two Dogs and one Little o'One Eyed Bear. And all a'us and o'Johnny, Papa said. But what got me Worried a'little, Calley said, is What we gonna do if one day Some Body comes a'riding by up on Top and Looks down and sees all these Horses we got down here. Why that'd be Hell to Pay and then Some wouldn't it, he said. We ain't never gonna let no body Hurt em, Annie said, if that's what you saying Mister Pearsall. No Ma'am I know we ain't, Calley said, but here's the Pickle. We ain't always down here to Look Out for em are we. Yes sir that is a Pickle ain't it I said, Papa said, and then Annie said I don't see why we don't just all move down here and live with Johnny and all them Horses so don't nothing Bad ever even get a Chance to come up. I like that Idea my self, Papa said, We'd be living in a'Hide Out like Real Out Laws wouldn't we. We are Real Out Laws Mister, Calley said, or ain't you been paying a'tention to What we been a'doing. We ain't so Bad I said, Papa said, I reckon they's a'lot worster but when I said that, he said, Why o'Calley give me a Look that'd light a'Fire in the Wood Pile and said Yes Sir you tell em that when they drop a'Noose round our Neck and Kick o'Sister and Firefoot out from under us and Oh his Eyes just went to Swimming when he said it cause he seen us hanging there from a limb in his mine.

LATER,

Papa said, when we was down there at the River getting us a'drink a'water Annie said Mister Pearsall Loves you like you was his own Son did you know that. Yes I do Know that Annie, I said, And I love him like a'Daddy I never even had. It was the Idear a'losing you that made him cry. Well I was just talking, Papa said. I didn't mean nothing. You made him Cry, Annie said, Shame on you. I'm gonna have to be more careful bout what I say from here on ain't I, Papa said, It bout made me Cry too to see him Cry. Well it did me too, Annie said, I wouldn't never wanna lose you no moren he would. I'm just gonna keep my mouth shut bout being a'Out Law next time, Papa said, even if I am One. You ain't no more a'Out Law'n I am, Annie said. We just going round trying to help Mistreated Horses is all. And Stealing em to do it, Papa said. But I don't reckon Deep Down I'd wanna be no other way bout it would you Annie. No she said Not me neither. We just a Horse Family I reckon. And Oh, Papa said, when Annie said that I couldn't help it and just leaned over there and give her a Kiss on her Cheek and she give it back to me on my Mouth and Oh it bout took my breath a'way. And then, Papa said, Annie said Well if I didn't know it be fore I know it now. We in Love ain't we she said. Yes I guess we are Annie, Papa said. But I reckon we been in Love a long time any how. Well what you wanna do bout it Mister, Annie said. I don't know, Papa said, Let's not talk bout it right now. Maybe it's Time we went on and got Married, Annie said, The way I see it we gonna get Married some day any how. How bout we get o'Reverend Skeen from down there round Cranes Mill to do it. Oh Boy Hidy, Papa said, that might be a'little Tricky getting down there and back with out no body asking us what we been a'doing all this time. How bout we get o'Calley to do it for us. He ain't no Preacher is he, Annie said, That'd be a Surprise to me if he was. Well he's kind of a'Preacher, Papa said, What you ain't noticed. Well yes I guess he is, she said. I reckon he can do it good as any body can, Papa said, and I think I'd feel Better bout getting Married if my o'Amigo Calley Pearsall is the one a'doing it to me any how.

*T*HE FIRST THING O'CALLEY SEEN when we walked up from the River, Papa said, was me and Annie a'holding Hands. Oh, he said, I reckon I know what This is all a'bout. Not cause I see yall holding Hands there he said but cause a'What I see in your Eyes long with it. We Love one a'nother, Annie said. Oh I know that Annie, Calley said. I seen it coming long Time a'go that Day after the Storm. If they was some thing Fore Ordained in this World, he said, it was you two Jumping the Broom together one day. We don't wanna Jump no Broom, Papa said, we want you to be the One Marrys us down here in The Narrows after we go tell the Choats bout it. Oh and then, Papa said, why o'Calley reached over and put his Arms round both a'us like he was our o'Daddy. I ain't never been Honored like this in my Life, he said then wiped his Eye fore a Tear could leak out. I bet this is the first time you ever cried two times in One Day in all your Life ain't it Mister Pearsall, Annie said. No Ma'am, he said, when the Tonks stole my little Dog out from under the Porch I Cried two days straight without Eating or Sleeping. That's bout the Saddest Story I ever did hear, Papa said. Well I ain't gonna tell it a'gain if that's what you worried bout, Calley said. Now where you reckon you gonna get some Words to go long with the Marriage, Annie said. I don't want no Jokes. And Oh we just went to Laughing bout it, Papa said, cause that'd be just like o'Calley wouldn't it. Annie looked over at me, he said, and said How bout you You got Any Thing in particular you want him to say and I said No I ain't even sure I'm gonna be there that day.

. . . where you reckon you gonna get some Words to go long with the Marriage, Annie said. I don't want no Jokes.

*N*EXT MORNING,
Papa said, me and Annie rode over to the Choats to give em the News but Oh
they was already a'standing out there in front a'the House a'clapping they
hands Hoo Ray Hoo Ray when we rode up. Bird must a'tole yall huh I said,
Papa said, but Miz Choat said Well he's the One said it but it was o'Jeffey
tole it. Then she come over and give us each a Hug and so did Marcellus and
Bird. Course it wadn't no Surprise to me to hear it, Miz Choat said. I believe
I could a'tole you the same thing my self with out no Help from o'Jeffey.
Well I didn't know it til Yesterday my self, Papa said. It just kind a'come
up on me of a Sudden I reckon. No, Miz Choat said, your o'Human Heart
been a'Whispering it to you all the Hours a'the Day and Night but you just
wadn't paying no a'tention til it reared back and Hollered in your Ear. She's
right, Mister Choat said. That's what happened to me. But it had to Holler at
you Two Three Four Hunderd Times fore you heared any thing at all Mister
Choat, she said, ain't that right. Well may be Miz Choat, Mister Choat said.
Then, Papa said, Marcellus said I think o'Jeffey got some thing to say here
and then Bird opened his Eyes and his Mouth so o'Jeffey could talk and she
said I ain't got nothing Special to say I just wanted to tell yall I'm Happy yall
found each other in this Life but they really wadn't never no Doubt bout
it. Oh and then big Tears come up in Annie's Eyes at what o'Jeffey said and
some more come up in mine cause I was Happy bout it too then Miz Choat
grabbed Annie by her Hand and took her in the House with her. Where they
going I said, Papa said, and Mister Choat said Miz Choat's gonna give her
the Talk since Annie ain't got no Momma to do it. What Talk's that you talking bout Mister Choat, Papa said, and Mister Choat said Let's you and me
go over here and set down a'minute in the Shade and I'll tell you. So, Papa
said, me and him went over there and set down under the Tree and Mister
Choat said I thought Mister Pearsall'd already tole you this fore now. Tole
me what, Papa said. Tole you bout Men and Women when they get Married
he said. No Sir, Papa said, he didn't tell me nothing. Well they ain't much to
it, Mister Choat said, here's all they is to know on your Wedding Night. Yes
Sir, Papa said, what's that. That o'Boy down there knows just what to Do,
Mister Choat said. All you got to do you self is just throw you Hat off and
Hang on.

$\mathcal{A}$BOUT THAT TIME,

Papa said, Annie put her Head out the Door and hollered Come look a'here at what Miz Choat give me and me and Mister Choat went on in the House with Marcellus and Bird and o'Fritz a'follering a'long behind. What is it Marcellus said and o'Jeffey said out Bird's Mouth I know what it is but I ain't a'telling. But what it was, Papa said, was a Dress been in Miz Choat's Trunk for bout a hunderd and six years. My Momma made it for me, she said, Ain't it Pretty. And now it's for you to get Married in same as I was if you like it Annie. Oh I do like it, Annie said, most specially cause you the One give it to me and then, Papa said, Annie did a'little Twirl round the room like she was back at Senora Garza's Place in San Antoneya a'Dancing on the Bar with Pela Rosa. Oh and then a Idea come to me for a Wedding Present for Annie, Papa said, and I went over there and whispered It to Mister Choat and Marcellus and asked em if they'd help me in Secret and not to tell Annie or no body else neither what it was and they both said Yes don't worry You got my Word on it Mister don't worry bout it. Then Mister Choat said, That's bout the nicest Present I ever heared a'some body coming up with for they Bride I wish I'd a'thought a'that for Hattie when we was both still Young and Limber like you two are now. Then he said Marcellus you better go to looking for you a Wife too so don't ever body in the Country get ahead a'you. I don't want no Wife, Marcellus said, and o'Jeffey said out Bird's mouth No Marcellus if you like ever other Man I ever knowed it ain't gonna be til after you got One that you don't want One no more. I wish I had a Wedding Ring to give you, Mister Choat said. The Ladies like they Wedding Rings you know it. Where yall gonna live any how he said and I said I don't think we decided yet. This all just come up. Well if yall don't wanna live at your Old Home Place you can move in here and live with us and we'd be Glad to have you he said. Well we got our Horse Busness to tend to, Papa said. I don't know how'd that work. Where is your Horse Busness at any how, Mister Choat said, you ain't said much bout it. Well we keeping some Horses down in The Narrows til we see what we gonna do with em, Papa said. Oh he give me a Look then and said You mean you Keeping em down there or You mean you a'Hiding em down there. Oh I didn't know what to answer, Papa said, but I knowed I wadn't gonna go to telling him Stories bout it so I just kind a'shuffled my Feet like I was squashing Bugs and didn't say nothing. The Reason I asked,

Mister Choat said, is theys People round here been a'missing some Horses and they getting fairly Irritated bout it and wanna do some thing to make it Stop and course what they talking bout is Hanging the Horse Theifs ever god dam One of em they can find he said.

WE WENT ON BACK TO THE NARROWS,

Papa said, and tole o'Calley bout Mister Choat asking if we was a'hiding Stole Horses down here in The Narrows and how I didn't answer one way or the other. The Question was bound to come up, Calley said, and they gonna be other Questions coming up too. Problem is, he said How we gonna answer em with out putting the Choats and o'Marcellus down in the Pickle Jar long with us. It is a Pickle ain't it, Annie said. If Mister and Miz Choat know what we doing, Calley said, and don't tell no body Why they inviting they own Hanging same as if they was Horse Theifs they self. Oh a Block a'Froze Ice went up my Back when o'Calley said that. What're we gonna do bout it, Papa said. We don't want no part a'getting the Choats in Trouble. O'Calley set down on the ground then, Papa said, and went to twirling his Spur like he done ever time he had some thing he needed to think bout. Ching e Ching e ChingChingChing Ching e Ching e ChingChingChing. Then of a sudden, Papa said, why o'Calley looked up and said I know what to do by god. Yes Sir Mister Pearsall what's that, Annie said, and he give us a Smile and said We just gonna let all them Horses go Just let em go and run a'way Free. You mean like they wadn't never ours in the First Place, Papa said. Well they wadn't never really ours in the First Place any how was they, Calley said, Hell we didn't Steal em We was just trying to Doctor em. They Stole they self more less didn't they, Annie said. Ain't that Right. Well some time they Stole each other I reckon, Papa said, but that still ain't us a'Stealing em is it. And we didn't never even try to Sell a'One of em neither did we So they can't put the Budge on us for that neither can they, Calley said. Just let em go huh, Annie said. Just set em a'loose to Run Free huh. They always been Free any how, Calley said, Free as a Bird. All they ever had to do was just Fly Off if they wanted to. Oh and then, Papa said, we looked over at the Big White Horse and Johnny and why they had they Ear cocked and was listening to ever Word we said. And it looked to me like Sister and o'Firefoot and ever other Horse down there was a'listening too, he said. You reckon they know what we a'Saying here, I said, Papa said, and Calley said Yes Sir and I think that ain't all Amigo I think they know what we a'Thinking too.

*F*RITZ AND O'POSSUM

and that little o'one eyed bear woke me up next Morning with they Howling and Crying bout some thing or other even fore the o'Sun come up, Papa said, and I looked over there and Why all the Horses was a'going up the side a'the Hill One by One and on out the top a'The Narrows and then, he said, Annie and o'Calley come a'wake and Annie said They a'leaving us for they own Life now ain't they. Yes Ma'am, Calley said, and I reckon they got ever Right they is to it sames we do ours. But then, Papa said, the Sun come up over there behind that Big White Horse in front and a'setting up there on top a'him like always wadn't no body in the World but o'Johnny. Hey Johnny where you a'going with all them Horses I hollered, Papa said, but he just give us a Smile and a'little wave Adios with his Flipper and run on off on the Big White Horse a'long with all them other Horses. All cept Firefoot, Papa said, and Sister and Annie's Horse Diamond. Where you reckon they a'going, Annie said. Just bout any wheres they wanna go, Calley said, then we run on up to the Top a'The Narrows our self, Papa said, and Oh there they went a'Galloping out cross the Country with o'Johnny and the Big White Horse Running out in Front. I never seen nothing so Pretty in all my Life as them Horses a'Running Free, Calley said, and Annie said Yes Sir and o'Johnny too. And then, Papa said, Calley said Yes Sir and o'Johnny too that's Right. You reckon we'll ever see em again, Papa said, I'm already Home Sick for em ain't you. Well Least we got to see em Running Free like that, Calley said, I reckon that's moren what most other People see in they whole Life Time. Theys a'nother Good Side to it too, Annie said, we can have our Marriage down here in The Narrows now if we want to cause we ain't Hiding Horses no more even if we didn't never Steal em in the First Place. I forgot to ask Miz Choat for some Words you could use at the Wedding if you needed em, Papa said. Want me to ride back over there and see if she got some. No, Calley said, I come up with a few Words a'my own that might do. Long as they ain't no Jokes in em, Annie said, I don't wanna start our new

Life together on a Joke Mister Pearsall. Well you should a'thought bout that fore you picked this Bohonk here for a Husband he said then laughed and give me a little Knock on my Head.

WELL I RECKON WE OUT A'THE HORSE BUSNESS now ain't we, Calley said. That didn't take long did it. Well, Papa said, we can always go in the Cow Busness, we ain't tried that yet. That's a good Idea Calley said Why they's Wild Cows all up and down the Blanco River and we can keep em down here in The Narrows same as we did the Horses. I don't see why not, Annie said. What was Good for the One oughta be Good for the Other. How much yall know bout the Cow Busness any how, she said. Catch em and Sell em is bout all I know, Calley said. I know a'little, Annie said. We can catch em and sell em or we can catch em and let em Grow us some more. You talking bout a'Ranch now ain't you Annie, Calley said. Yes I am, Annie said, I sure am. A Home and a Ranch, she said. I like that, Papa said. Well I like it too, o'Calley said, but you talking bout Setting Still in Just One Place ain't you Annie. Well that's what a Home and a'Ranch'd be Mister Pearsall, Annie said, I don't see how that'd hurt you any. I just don't know bout all that Setting in One Place is all, Calley said, I ain't sure I was made for that. You could always Up and Go if it turns out you don't like it, Annie said. No body's gonna try to Coop you up if that's what you a'thinking. No that ain't what I was thinking, Calley said, What I was thinking is Yall gonna want you own Life now and don't need me a'poking round in it ever Day. You wouldn't be in the Way Mister Pearsall, Annie said, we'd be Glad to have you. Yes Sir, Papa said, Glad. Course you can always run me off if it don't work out for you I reckon, Calley said. We wouldn't never do that in our Life, Papa said. No Sir not never. Well I reckon we can try it a'while, Calley said, but I'm gonna wanna fix me up a'Room in one a'the Stalls down there in the Barn so I ain't in the way. But you gonna take your Suppers with us, Annie said, we won't have it no other way Mister Pearsall. No Sir, Papa said, course we might be out there in the Country chasing cows most a'the Time any how. Well, Annie said, that's Settled. Now all we got to do is go on and get Married fore we too Old and Cripid to do it.

I RODE BACK OVER TO THE CHOATS

after that, Papa said, and tole em we was gonna have the Marriage down there in The Narrows it was so Pretty and o'Jeffey said out Bird's Mouth she liked that Idea cause she was too Big when she was a'Live to get down there and back up a'gain with out some o'Mule a'carrying her and she always hoped to see it. Mister Choat said Well I guess they ain't no Horses down in there to get in the way Huh and I said, Papa said, No Sir they Ain't no Horses down in there cep our own. Then I tole em how we was gonna go up and down the Blanco River and catch all the Wild Cows we could find and start us a'Cow Ranch. I always knowed you was gonna be a Cow Boy, Miz Choat said, but maybe it's just that John B Stetson Hat you been a'wearing. I reckon I'd wanna be a Cow Boy even if I wadn't wearing a'John B, Papa said, but I used to wanna Blow a'Horn in the Dance Band from that Time we was all over there at Fischer Hall and ever body was a'Dancing To and Fro. Mister Choat's always been a good Dancer his self, Miz Choat said, cep he only Dances up and down in one Spot like some body nailed his feet down. Oh Hattie you just always a'talking ain't you, Mister Choat said. Then Marcellus said We been working on that Wedding Present you wanted us to make for Annie you wanna go down to the Barn and see how we doing on it. So we went down there and Oh it was xactly what I been hoping it was gonna be. It couldn't be no Better, I said. Where you want us to put it, Mister Choat said. You didn't say nothing bout that. I'd like to put it out there in the Front Yard up at the House and then put some chairs on the Porch where ever body can set and watch. Annie ain't got no Idea bout it does she, Miz Choat said. Its gonna Surprise her ain't it. I know it would me. Marcellus, Mister Choat said, let's don't forget to hang a couple a'Lanterns out there on the Porch so ever body can get a good Look when Annie goes to using it.

*C*OUPLE A'DAYS LATER,

Papa said, we all went down to The Narrows for our Marriage cep Mister Choat and Marcellus who was taking my Wedding Present over to the House where Annie wouldn't know and they was Late getting to The Narrows. Where yall been, Annie said in Miz Choat's pretty Wedding Dress. Didn't no body ever tell yall we was having a Wedding here to Day. We just had some thing we had to do but we done it and we here now, Mister Choat said then went over there and give Bird a'Kiss cause he looked so Pretty with all them Flowers Miz Choat put in his hair. Then, Papa said, I stepped over there and took a'holt a'Annie's Hand and she said Where you at Mister Pearsall we ready here now. Oh and then here come o'Calley out from over there some wheres and he had his Boots shined and his Hair Combed back like a Barber done it and he said I'm ready if yall are and me and Annie said Yes Sir we are. Then, Papa said, why ever body come a'Crowding in close to where we was and Calley looked at Us and said Yall come here to get Married today is that Right then he squinted his Eyes like he was a'Testing me and said Do you Love this Woman here Mister and I said Yes Sir I do Love this Woman here. And then, Papa said, he give Annie the same Look and said Ma'am do you Love this Man here and Annie said Oh Yes Sir I do Love this Man here same as he Loves me. And Yall both sure bout it, he said, yall still got Time if yall wanna think bout it a'nother two three years. And then Annie give him a Mean look for his Joke and said No Sir we sure bout it. Then we squeezed our Hands together cause we both Meant ever Word we said, Papa said. Well, Calley said, Well that's what Marriage is ain't it. It's Love ever Day the rest a'your Life til Kingdom Come. A Men Miz Choat said A Men Mister Choat said A Men o'Marcellus said. Then, Papa said, here come one more A Men out Bird's mouth but it was from o'Jeffey over yonder on the Other Side where she was. Oh and then we looked up, Papa said, and Why up there on the Top a'The Narrows was o'Johnny a'setting on that Big White Horse and all round em was all them other Horses been Mistreated and they was just a'Nodding they Head and a'Stomping they Feet like this was the Prettiest Wedding they ever been to in they Life and o'Johnny tried to clap his Hands together cause he liked it so much too but No they just wouldn't reach. And then o'Calley wiped his Eye and put both his Arms round me and Annie and pulled us over close. Yall Husband and Wife now, he said, I don't believe neither one a'you could a'Chose no better in this World. Then Miz Choat give us a Hug too and so did Mister Choat and so did o'Marcellus and then if that wadn't enough, Papa said, why here come Fritz and o'Possum and that poor Little o'One Eyed Bear to give us Licks and Grins cause they was so Happy bout ever thing too. I liked your Ceremony Mister Pearsall, Miz Choat said. Thank you Miz Choat, Calley said. I was fraid I was talking too Long but I didn't know how I could cut it down no further.

104

after that, Papa said, so we all got on our Horse and rode on back to the House for Grape Juice and so Annie could see her Wedding Present out there in the Front Yard where Mister Choat and Marcellus put it. What is it, Annie said, but Miz Choat tole her to squeeze her Eyes shut so she couldn't see nothing then led her out on the Front Porch and said Ever Body Ready and, Papa said, we all said Yes Ma'am We Ready and Miz Choat said Okay Annie open your Eyes now and Annie did but at First she didn't see nothing cause my Wedding Present was a'laying flat down on the Ground to where couldn't No Body hardly see it but then of a sudden, Papa said, she did see it then looked over at me and said Oh is that what I think it is. Well you just gonna have to go See if it is or not Annie, I said, Papa said, and Annie jumped off the Porch and give it a'nother Look and said Oh Yes It Is Yes Yes It Is and then next thing she just went to Dancing on it cause what it was Was a bunch a'wood boards put together to make her a'Dance Floor she could Dance on any time she wanted to just like if she was still back in Senora Garza's Place down in San Antoneya a'Dancing on the Bar. Oh she did like it, Papa said, and right a'way went to Twirling on it and Singing a'Song she knowed bout a'Dreamer. And then in a minute she come up on the Porch and made me go out there and Dance on it with her but, Papa said, I was shy bout Dancing in front a'People and just stood there grinning like a Knot on a Log I reckon but then Mister Choat come out the House with some o'Fiddle he had hid up under the Bed or some where and hollered Bride and Groom Dance Bride and Groom Dance and ever body started a'Laughing and a'Hollering Bride and Groom Dance Bride and Groom Dance too and they wadn't nothing I could do but go on and Dance with my Bride best I could and while we was a'Dancing I looked up there and I seen o'Calley setting in a chair kind a'watching us but mostly just a'Twirling his Spur Ching e Ching e ChingChingChing and I knowed no matter how Happy he was for me and Annie he couldn't help but wish it was him and Pela Rosa a'Dancing out there on that Dance Floor in sted. Then I guess Miz Choat seen it too, Papa said, cause she went over there and tole him to come on and Dance with her and she wadn't gonna let him say No and Oh they Danced up a'Storm and then Miz Choat went over there and asked Marcellus for a Dance too and Oh Boy Hidy, he said, o'Marcellus jumped right up and went to Dancing like may be he been a'Practicing how to Dance in Secret ever day a'his Life. And course all this Time o'Fritz was just a'Yipping and a'going round in Circles to the Music like he was trying to Dance too, Papa said, and so was that Little o'One Eyed Bear but he took up too much room on the Dance Floor and Miz Choat had to give him a little pop on his Hiney with a Stick to run him back out in the yard where o'Possum was a'taking him a Good Nap.

*O*H WE DANCED AND WE DANCED and we danced, Papa said, til ever body was all Wore Out from it and went to Sleep out there on the Front Porch with Fritz and Possum and that Little o'One Eyed Bear and then me and Annie Sneaked on in the House just by our self And Oh we was Glad to do it, he said.

*C*OUPLE A'TWO THREE DAYS LATER, Papa said, me and o'Calley started our Cow Busness cause we didn't have no more Time to Fool Round and that First Day we come out a'the Brush with two three Wild Cows and the next day another One but the Coyotes already made a Steer out a'him when he was just a little Fella. But we was on our way, he said, and Annie was Happy we was so good at what we was a'doing. Then the next day after that, Papa said, we was a'riding cross this Hill and Oh we seen this Herd a'Horses a'running way out yonder and it looked like it was o'Johnny a'riding up in front on the Big White Ghost Horse. That's o'Johnny on the Big White Horse ain't it I said, Papa said, and Calley said Yes Sir I do believe it is and it looks to me like they been stealing some more Mistreated Horses cause they's moren they was last time we seen em ain't they. I didn't never count em Papa said, but Yes Sir looks like it to me too. I bet they's a'Bunch a'People after em for it too don't you. Oh Yes Sir, Calley said, then had to pull o'Firefoot up some cause he wanted to go down there and Run with em too. I guess he's remembering the Good o'Days when he was out there a'running with em ain't he huh, Papa said. And then o'Firefoot jumped a'gain and Calley bout lost his seat this time. Whoa Whoa, Calley said, then climbed down off Firefoot and walked round to give him a Look in his Eye. What's wrong with you Mister, he said, it ain't like you to be some

106

Oh we danced and we danced and we
danced, Papa said, til ever body
was all Wore Out from it . . .

o'Smarty Pants like this but Firefoot tryed to look some wheres else so Calley couldn't give him that Look but, Papa said, o'Calley kep his Eye right on him til Firefoot give up what ever it was he was a'thinking and Shook his self clear of it. Is they Some thing wrong with o'Firefoot, Papa said, and Calley said He's trying to listen to two Voices both at the same time but he ain't quite able to do it and it's making him Fidgitty. Who else he a'trying to listen to sides you, Papa said, I don't see no body else round here. Well if I was a'saying, Calley said, I'd say it's that Big White Horse is the One a'trying to talk to him and not no body else. What you reckon he wants to Talk to him bout, Papa said and Calley said Oh I know xactly what bout. It's bout going out there with all them other Horses and a'Running Free. O'Firefoot wouldn't never leave you and do that would he Calley, Papa said, and Calley said Well would you if you was a Horse. And then, Papa said, I looked down at Sister and I could tell she was a'wanting to go down there and Run too.

A'NOTHER DAY SOME TIME LATER,

Papa said, me and Calley and Annie and the Dogs and that Little Bear was coming back to the House with one o'Cow we just caught out the Brush and here come four Men a'riding up with they Big Guns ready. We looking for Horse Theifs they said Yall seen any and Calley said No Sir we a'looking for Maverick Cows Yall seen any a'them. No Sir, the Man said. These Horse Theifs we a'looking for is Horses they self you ever heared such a thing like that in your Life. I reckon some body just a'pulling your Leg Mister, Annie said, you ever think bout that. No Listen here, he said, they come up to my Place here the other day and stole some a'mine in Broad Day Light so I seen it my self I ain't just telling Stories here. Well we ain't seen em, Papa said, we just out here looking for Wild Cows. They's a little Funny Looking Man rides with em on a Big White Horse, the Man said. Ever body in the Country is out trying to Shoot him. Well not ever body, one a'the other Men said, them Horse Theifs rode right up to Old Man Cagle's Place and didn't steal a'one a'his Horses even if they was bout twenty or so right there in his Pen. Mister Cagle must be a pretty good Fella when it comes to how he treats his Horses then huh, Calley said. I don't know what that got to do with it Mister, the Man said. Just sounds like to me them Horse Theifs you talking bout here Picks and Chooses what Horses they gonna steal, Calley said, and don't want none that's already got em a Good Home. Yes Sir sounds like that to me too, Papa said, then Annie said Yes Sir me too and the Man give us a look and said What are yall a Bunch a'Lutherins from up yonder round Johnson City some wheres. No Sir we just don't like seeing a Horse Mistreated is all, Calley said, I reckon that's the kind a'People we are. I don't know if that's Lutherin or not. Oh and then, Papa said, the Man give Calley the Snake Eyes cause he didn't know was Calley trying to pick a Fight with him or was he just a'Talking. Well they's plenty a'us on the Hunt for them Horse Theifs even if yall ain't, the Man said. Well we ain't, Calley said, so you at least got that Part right. But, Papa said, he said it with a little Smile so the Man could take Offense or Not which ever way he wanted. Then they rode on off, Papa said, and I said I'm worried bout o'Johnny and Annie said Yes I am too and o'Calley said Well he ain't never coming back to us any how cause now o'Johnny done cast his Lot with the Horses like maybe they was his Brothers and Sisters after all.

ANNIE DIDN'T FEEL MUCH LIKE DANCING that night, Papa said, but went on out there on the Dance Floor any how and Danced to perk us up after being so Scared and Gloomy bout o'Johnny. Well we was talking one time bout how ever body gets to Pick they own Life, Calley said. I reckon this is the One o'Johnny picked for his self cause I don't see how some body else could a'picked it for him do you. I don't know how he could a'picked it for his self, Annie said. Poor o'Johnny can just barely ty his own shoes. He can ride a Horse, Papa said, Why I never seen the Like in my Life. I didn't mean nothing by it, Annie said, I was just talking. I know it, Papa said, I didn't mean nothing neither. It's out a'our Hands any how, Calley said, How you gonna tell a'bunch a'Horses to Stop what they doing fore some body Shoots em for it. I don't believe they'd care even if some body does Shoot em for it, Annie said. Looks to me like they gonna do what they gonna do til they get done a'doing it and ain't no body else got a'thing to say bout it. Well I reckon this is just the Life they chose too then ain't it huh Calley, Papa said, and Calley said You gonna have to ask some body else bout that I don't know ever thing in the World but we got Horses stealing

Horses now so I don't reckon nothing else much gonna Surprise me from here on out in my Life. I just want em to be Safe, Annie said. I know Annie, Calley said, but we don't always get what we Want do we. Well I did, Annie said, and give me a Look to show she was talking bout me. And I give her that look right back, Papa said, to show her I did too. If yall don't quit all this Monkeying round, Calley said, I'm gonna go to Town first thing in the Morning and sell yall both to the Circus when it comes through. If they'll take you, he said, and Oh, Papa said, we got a big Laugh out a'that sames we did from just bout ever thing else that ever come out his Mouth.

*N*EXT MORNING FIREFOOT WAS GONE, Papa said, and Calley said it's all my Fault I knowed that Big White Horse put the Idea in his Head but I got Lazy and didn't lock the god dam Barn Door. Where you reckon he went, Papa said, and Calley said I don't Reckon Amigo I know. He's gone with all them other Horses. Why'd he go and do that, Papa said, he got a good Home here don't he. The Home he's a'Looking for ain't on a'piece a'Ground, Calley said, it's way down deep in his Heart. We gonna go find him ain't we, Papa said, and Calley said We sure gonna try Mister. Then, Papa said, Calley throwed his Saddle up on Annie's Horse Diamond and I did mine up on o'Sister and Annie give us some Eats in a sack she made for our Trip. How long yall gonna be gone, she said, and Calley said Just ain't no way a'knowing Annie might be a short time might be a long time. Don't worry Annie, Papa said, We gonna be back just soons we can you can count on that. Oh and then she blowed me a little Kiss, Papa said, and I blowed her one back then we trotted on off with Fritz and o'Possum a'follering long behind like a'couple a'Track Dogs which a'course they wadn't. And then, he said, that Little o'One Eyed Bear put up a Fuss bout it cause he wanted to go too but No we wanted him to stay there with Annie cause if some body come round needed to be Run off why he could sure do the Job. I'm gonna miss Annie I said, Papa said, this is bout the First Time we been a'part moren a'Day since we got Married you know it. Yes I do know it, Calley said, If you recall Mister I was the one said the Words there at your Marriage that day. Course I remember it, Papa said, you talked bout

Loving each other didn't you but o'Calley just nodded and didn't say nothing back. You miss Pela Rosa some time don't you Calley, Papa said. No Sir not just Some Time, Cally said, all the god dam Time. That's Hard huh, Papa said. I hope you don't never have to live through nothing like it Amigo, Calley said, It'll break you Heart in two and they ain't no wheres to go for Help I know of cep maybe your Guardian Angel but she ain't hardly never paying a'tention so you out a'Luck there too ain't you. It's that Bad huh, Papa said. Yes it is, Calley said, Yes it is. You ain't gonna die from it are you Calley, Papa said, but Calley give Diamond his Heels and just trotted on off cause he didn't wanna talk bout it no more.

*I*T TOOK ME A'MINUTE, Papa said, but I caught up to him. You ain't gonna are you I said. Ain't gonna What, Calley said. Ain't gonna die from it, Papa said. I was just talking, Calley said, you got a Bad Habit a'listening to ever Word I say. Are they always there, Papa said. Are who always there, Calley said. Them Guardian Angels you was talking bout when you a'missing Pela Rosa. Why, Calley said, you need to talk to some o'Angel. I still miss my Momma, Papa said, and now I miss my Brother Herman too. I can't say I know for sure, Calley said, but Yes I reckon Angels is always there to open the Door when you Knock. Is that what you do, Papa said. O'Calley pulled up cause he seen I just wadn't gonna let it go. What I do, he said, is I make a'Pitchur in my Head a'this Door. A'Door to where, Papa said. Just a Door it don't matter Where to, Calley said. You wanna hear this or not Amigo. Yes Sir, Papa said. So I make a Pitchur a'this Door in my Head, Calley said, then I reach up there and Knock on it and I say Hello I'm standing out here all by my self and could use me a Friend if you Please cause I lost my Sweet Heart and I'm a'grieving some thing awful for her and it's bout to drive me Crazy. And then some body comes on out huh, Papa said. No, Calley said, but I get this Feeling like you walking through a'Cold Room one night and then you walk by the Fire over there and for just a'minute you never been so Warm in all you whole Life as you are right then and you know you gonna be alright long as you can walk by that Fire. Is the Fire that Angel you was talking bout, Papa said. I don't know Who or What it is, Calley said. I just get the Feeling it's some body there wants to Help me cause I asked em to. And when you been feeling Ice Cold bout things like I been feeling bout Pela Rosa, he said, you glad to get a Warm Feeling any wheres you can find one. Some night when you missing you Momma and you Brother, Calley said, you might wanna reach up and knock on that Door you self and see what happens. I ain't always been Good, Papa said, I don't reckon some o'Angel gonna wanna Help me any how. From what I know, Calley said, Angels is just there to Help when some body asks for some. It ain't like they got a Horse in the Race they self.

OH WE LOOKED AND WE LOOKED ALL DAY LONG, Papa said, but we couldn't never even pick up Firefoot's Tracks. May be he sprouted Wings and just Flew off some wheres I said. Or may be he didn't never even come this way any how, Calley said. Only way we gonna find him is to find o'Johnny and them other Horses first cause that's where he's a'gonna go don't you reckon. Yes Sir I do reckon it, Papa said, I don't know what else I'd reckon bout it any how. Oh and then that Afternoon, he said, we come up on this Dead Horse been Shot through the Neck and they was Horse Tracks ever wheres you looked from where a'Bunch a'Horses been Running to get a'way if they could and four a'them tracks was Firefoot's. He's with em, Calley said. And I could tell he was Worried Sick bout it too. Who you figgur killed this Pretty Horse here, Papa said, and Calley got off Diamond and follered some Horse Tracks went off in a'Direction all by they self. Lets foller and see Where they go he said and So, Papa said, we went a'Sneaking long and then just bout Dark we seen these Men a'getting off they Horses way out there to make em a Camp for the Night and one of em was a'riding a Black Horse and Oh that Man was Sheriff Simon Pugh from San Antoneya and I knowed it was him, Papa said, cause I seen the Wind lift his Hair up off that little Black Dot that was his Ear Hole. It's o'Sheriff Pugh I said, Papa said, Remember him. Oh and then o'Calley went Red in his Face and give Sheriff Pugh the Snake Eyes even if he was bout a'Hunderd and One Miles off cause he was the one Shot and Killed Pela Rosa that Day and o'Calley wadn't never gonna forget it til the day he died and probably not even then neither. What's he want round here, Papa said. Him and his Possee is a'looking for them Horse Theifs like ever body else in the Country, Calley said. He wants to Catch em and Make a'Name for his Self all up and down the Country. The Funny Thing, he said, is o'Sheriff Pugh don't have no Idea his own Little Brother is one of em. He ain't gonna think that's Funny when he finds out is he, Papa said. No Sir and I don't think it's Funny nei-ther, Calley said, cause that Son of a Bitch gonna Shoot First and see What At later and that scares me for o'Johnny don't it you. Yes Sir, Papa said. Yes Sir it does. And it Scares me for o'Firefoot too, Calley said, And for all them other Horses too and I said Oh Yes Sir Yes Sir me too. But they was just too many Men down there in the Sheriff's Possee for just us to Fight so we turned round and went on back in the Direction we come from so o'Sheriff Pugh wouldn't know we even been there in the First Place.

O THAT NIGHT

when I was a'trying to go to Sleep I made a Pitchur in my Mine a'this Door like o'Calley said he did some time and then I reached up there and Knocked on it and said Hello Hello I'm standing out here all by my self in the Dark and would like to say Hidy to my Momma and my Brother Herman Please but I didn't hear nothing back. So, he said, I Knocked a'gain but No, Papa said, nothing come back to me a'gain So I Knocked a'gain and a'gain and a'gain in case they wadn't no body heared me the First Time but then of a sudden this Warm Feeling come up all over me just like o'Calley said come over him some time like he was in a Cold Room and walked by the Fire. And Oh, Papa said, it give you the nicest Feeling you ever did have in your Life so I got close to it as I could and went on off to sleep a'feeling Good bout ever thing but then here in a minute it give me a'Lick on my Face and I said Wait a minute this ain't no Angel this is a Dog Lick and Oh turned out it wadn't just one Dog Lick but was Two cause Fritz and o'Possum was both in bed with me now. Then I said to myself, Papa said, Well this didn't work out like o'Calley said it would But then I said Well may be it did work too cause now I got a Good Feeling them Dogs getting in Bed with me like this and may be it was my Momma and my Brother Herman put em up to it to let me know they was a'Thinking bout me same Time I was a'Thinking bout them. I was wide a'wake now, he said, and of a sudden I heared a Horse snort and looked over there and Oh here come Firefoot out the Dark just a'Tip Toeing over to Calley and put his Nose down to him like he was a'trying to Whisper some thing in his Ear while he was a'sleeping like that and Oh I said to my self, Papa said, Why look a'there o'Firefoot come to say Hidy to his o'Amigo Calley Pearsall didn't he. But then, Papa said, it come to me No o'Firefoot wadn't here to say Hidy he was here to say Adios Amigo.

*N*EXT DAY WE WENT OUT A'LOOKING A'GAIN, Papa said, but we didn't see nothing and no body til late in the Day and then there was all them Horses way out yonder just a'running cross the Country like a'big Dust Storm been cut a'loose and a'Running up in front with o'Johnny and that Big White Horse was o'Firefoot his self. Oh it was so Pretty all them Horses a'Running Free like that Why me and Calley both pulled up and just set there a'watching em. You gonna go a'long Time fore you see any thing Pretty as that a'gain ain't you, Calley said, and I said Yes Sir ain't you, Papa said. And then I ask him how many Horses he figgured was in that Bunch now and he said he didn't rightly know but may be some wheres round Three Four Hunderd or so and may be moren that But it was hard to tell how many cause they was Kicking up so much Dust wadn't they. And I'll tell you one more god dam thing, Calley said, I never seen o'Firefoot Happier bout some thing in all his Life. Oh and then I looked over and seen Calley's Eyes just a'Dancing at how much he liked seeing Firefoot a'Running Free like that with all them others. You ain't gonna try to catch him now are you Calley, Papa said. No Sir not today, Calley said. And probably not never neither. So we just set there, Papa said, and watched em Run on off til o'Johnny up there on the Big White Horse wadn't no moren just a'little fat Sausage a'going out cross the Country. Then we turned o'Sister and Diamond round and went to looking for Wild Cows a'gain and so did o'Possum but Fritz jumped up in front a'me on the Saddle cause he didn't hardly never wanna Walk if they was a Chance he could Ride.

But then, Papa said, it come to me No o'Firefoot wadn't here to say Hidy he was here to say Adios Amigo.

I RECKON IT WAS THREE FOUR DAYS LATER
we got Home with three more Wild Cows, Papa said, and it was like me and
Annie hadn't a'seen each other in a'Year and a'Half and Oh we was so Glad
to be together a'gain. I was so Worried bout you I was bout to climb on this
Little Bear here and come a'looking for You my self, she said. Well I'd a'liked
to seen that, Papa said, you a'riding that Bear. And Annie said Well you stay
Gone this long next time you are gonna see it Mister. Oh we Laughed, Papa
said, and we was a'needing us a Laugh too and then we set down at the Table
for our Suppers and Annie said they was two Men from Blanco come by here
the other day when yall was gone and they wanted to know was those Cows
we got down in the Pen for Sale and I said No Sir we building a'Cow Ranch
here and they's our Start but we gonna have some Cows for Sale later on and
Yall can come on back and buy em then. That's right, Calley said, we don't
never wanna run no body off if they might turn out to be a Buyer. And Oh,
Papa said, Annie was Proud Calley thought she done right and I was too but
it didn't surprise me a'Lick she had. Then, Annie said, them Men said they
been in to Blanco the other day and the Sheriff a'San Antoneya Texas was in
Blanco too the same time they was and he was offering a Cash Reward for
some body to catch that Big White Horse and that Man a'Riding him cause
they was stealing Horses all over the Place and couldn't no body catch em.
A Reward, Calley said. Yes Sir a Reward, Annie said. Dead or A'Live. Dead or
A'Live, Papa said. Dead or A'Live. Didn't a'one a'us say any thing for a good
long time, Papa said, then Calley said If I knowed how to go warn Johnny
and Firefoot and that Big White Horse bout it I would but I reckon if we was
to go a'Chasing after em to tell em Why they'd just run on off and wouldn't
never stop to listen any how would they. This is Bad Pookie we got here ain't
it, he said, Bad Bad Pookie. So we just set there at the table for bout a'year
a'looking at one a'nother and then of a sudden it come to me, Papa said, If
we went to Chasing em and they wouldn't in no way Stop and let us catch
up to em Why then may be we could Chase em clear out this Country round
here to some other Country where they wadn't no body a'trying to Murder
em. I believe I got the Smartest Husband in Town ain't I, Annie said, and
Calley said Least we can try it I reckon by god. I'm going with you this time,
Annie said, yall ain't leaving me here.

*W*E LET OUR COWS A'LOOSE

so they wouldn't starve to Death in the Pens while we was gone, Papa said, and then Calley climbed up on o'Diamond and me and Annie went double on Sister and then Triple if you count when o'Fritz jumped up on there with us. And then, he said, course o'Possum and that Little o'One Eyed Bear follered long behind like they was Trackers. I don't know what I'd do if I looked up and seen some thing like Us a'coming up the Road, Calley said, I might just run for the Hills. Well I said to my self, Papa said, this might not be such a Hard Trip as I thought it was gonna be if o'Calley is gonna crack a'Joke ever step a'the way like this. But No I was wrong, he said, cause bout the next step we took here come the Sheriff a'Blanco County o'Pie Jones and some Man there with him both bout covered up with Ropes to go catch some thing or other with. I believe yall got a Bear a'follering you did you know that o'Sheriff Pie Jones said. Yes Sir, Papa said, he follers us ever wheres we go. For what Reason the Sheriff said and I said I don't know I reckon you just gotta ask him. What happened to his Eye, the other Man said. Looks like he got one Missing don't he. Yes Sir, Papa said, a Bad Man poked it out for him over in San Antoneya with a Pointy Stick one day. The Hell you say, the Sheriff said, I'm surprised he could get close nough to him to do it. Did you see it when he did it he said and Papa said No Sir I didn't and then the Sheriff said Why not You ain't Blind too are you and Oh then, Papa said, the Sheriff and that other Man both just went to Laughing bout it. I wadn't there is Why I didn't see it, Papa said, or I reckon I would a'seen it. You wanna see things in this World you gotta keep you Eyes open, the Sheriff said, you know that. He just tole you he wadn't there Mister, Annie said, you ain't got a Bug in your Ear have you. But, Papa said, Annie said it so low o'Sheriff Pie Jones couldn't hardly hear it and said What's that you say Ma'am and Oh then Annie fairly shouted I SAID YOU GOT A BUG IN YOUR EAR OR WHAT. And I thought Oh Boy Hidy we in Trouble now ain't we, Papa said, but No he give Annie a Smile and tipped his Hat Adios. I'm sorry Ma'am he said but me and o'Leonard just ain't got time for a Joke right now then him and his Friend rode on off. See all them ropes on they Saddle, Calley said, they going out after Johnny and that Big White Horse to get the Reward ain't they. Like ever body else, he said.

117

ONCET WE FIND EM,

Annie said, where we gonna Run em off to where can't no body ever find em a'gain. I'm thinking West some wheres in the Mountains, Calley said, I reckon they'd like that Country and they ain't many People out there to Mistreat em as they are here any how. I might even like to Live out there with em my self, he said. It's a Pretty Country all round. You ever been out there Mister Pearsall, Annie said. I spent some Time out there in my Youth, Calley said, but it didn't a'mount to much. I never knowed that, Papa said, I reckon you been a'keeping Secrets huh. I come close to going Bad out there is Why. But I don't wanna Talk bout it, he said, I'd just be giving my self a Bad Reputation and they's plenty a'other People already a'doing that for me ain't they. What'd you do Rob a Bank, Annie said. You can tell us we ain't gonna tell no body. No Ma'am I didn't Rob no Bank, Calley said, they ain't nothing to buy out there any how I know of. So what'd you do Calley, Papa said. Well, he said, if I was to tell you You wouldn't go tell some body else would you. No Sir Annie said. No Sir Papa said. I didn't Rob no Bank, Calley said. Okay, me and Annie said, Papa said, So who'd you Rob then. I Robbed a'Priest, Calley said, I robbed a'Priest right there in his own Church House. You Robbed a'Priest, Annie said. Oh I don't know bout you Mister Pearsall. And I'd do it a'gain he said. They was this Poor Mexkin Family out there didn't have two pennys they could rub together but they had this little Sick Boy name a'Crecencio crawled round on the ground cause one a'his Legs was born bout half a'Arm shortern the other one and Oh it was just awful to see Poor Little Crecencio a'trying to get round on it like that so one day I tole his Momma and Daddy I was sorry to see the Fix they Little Boy was in but they said No the Priest is a'talking to God bout getting both his Legs the same size but God told the Priest Don't Worry he's gonna get round to it just soon as they give him some Money for his work. I said What, Calley said, that Priest is a'wanting you to pay God for what God supposed to be a'doing in the First Place and they said Si Senyor and we been Glad to do it ever since. So I went over to that Priest, Calley said, and said How you getting that Money up to God you been taking off these Poor People here for they Little Boy's Short Leg and the Priest said Oh Don't Worry Senyor I been getting it up to him and I said Well he tole me he ain't been getting it and wants me to get it for him and then, Calley said, I showed him my Big o'Pistola and tole him if I was ever to hear a'such a'god dam thing a'gain in my Life why I was

118

gonna send him up there his self to see what God got to say to him bout do-ing Things like this. And far as I Know, he said, that pretty much Broke that Son of a Bitch a'the Habit.

$\mathcal{E}$VER WHERES WE WENT,
Papa said, they was People out a'Looking for Johnny and the Big White Horse. Course, he said, they didn't have no Idea who o'Johnny was or where he come from in the First Place and went to calling him the Ghost Rider cause they couldn't think a'nothing no better and cause when they seen him he was going so fast he wadn't hardly no moren a'Blur a'going cross the Country on that Big White Horse with Firefoot and all them other Horses a'Running a'long behind and more coming ever Day. They like a'Storm a'Blowing cross the Land ain't they, Annie said, and I said I ain't never heared it put no better have you Calley and Calley said No Sir not me nei-ther. But the Trouble was, Papa said, we couldn't find em to drive em on West to a Safe Place where couldn't no body Catch em or Shoot em. I wish one a'these Dogs here was a Horse Tracker, Calley said, but I don't reckon neither one of em could find a Horse even if they was a'setting there in the Saddle they self. And it was bout then, Papa said, that here come three Men from up the Road and Oh they was bout all wore out and they Horses was too and we knowed Why too. Yall been a'Chasing that Ghost Rider and the Big White Horse ain't you, Calley said. Yes Sir Chased em from Hell to Breakfast and Back the Head Man said, and ain't never gonna chase em a'gain neither. We was Five when we started out, he said, but they's only just Three a'us left now. Where'd the other Two go, Papa said. We buried em back yonder a'ways so they Family's wouldn't have to see what they looked like after that Bunch a'god dam Horses run back and forth over em like that, the Man said. I'm sorry, Calley said, I reckon them Horses was just trying to protect they self wadn't they. Call it what ever you want Mister, the Man said, I reckon ever body else gonna call it Murder. Then the Man tried to spit on the ground but he was so dry nothing come out, Papa said, and they went on off. Murder, Annie said, But What bout how all them Horses been Bad Mistreated they self. Who you gonna find round here ever gonna believe what a Horse got to say any how Calley said.

*T*HEN WE STARTED FINDING DEAD HORSES
right a'long bout ever wheres we went, Papa said, and o'Calley could hardly
stand it cause he was fraid the next one was gonna be o'Firefoot his self but
we just kep a'going, he said, even if we was Heart Sick bout seeing all these
Horses been Shot Dead long the way. I reckon you bout ready to go Home
ain't you Annie, Calley said. This ain't no place for a'Tender Heart is it. I ain't
no Tender Heart, she said, I'm a Married Woman and I stay with my Husband ever wheres he goes and ain't no body gonna tell me different Mister
Pearsall. I wadn't trying to Annie, o'Calley said, I was just remarking on the
Situation. Don't try to run me off cause you Scared a'what I might see on
this Trip, Annie said, I ain't a'going Home and you can't make me. Why Annie I wouldn't try to make you do any thing in the World you didn't wanna
do he said. I know you got a mine a'your own. And then Oh, Papa said, we
seen all them Horses Way Way Out Yonder a'weaving back and forth cross
the Country like Birds do some times up in the Sky. They already headed
West on they own ain't they, Papa said, and Calley said Yes Sir let's just keep
em a'going that way and Not let em turn back on us if we can help it. Then
he Whooped and went to Waving his John B up in the Air and me and Annie
did too and Oh we did give Chase, Papa said, and Why you never seen any
thing like it in all you Life all three a'us just a'Running and a'Jumping after
o'Johnny and that Big White Horse and Firefoot and all them other Horses
too and Fritz and o'Possum and that Little o'One Eyed Bear just a'Running
Running Running to keep up if they could and Annie's arms round my middle like a'nother part a'me. Oh Listen here Mister, he said, you just couldn't
ask for no Better.

*T*HAT EVENING,
Papa said, all them Horses stopped at a Creek to get em a Drink a'Water and
we did too But, he said, o'Johnny and that Big White Horse and o'Firefoot
too stayed over there by they self to keep Watch on ever body else. They
like some Big o' Daddys a'watching over they Family ain't they, Annie said,
I never would a'thought o'Johnny'd ever come round to being some thing
like this. So, Papa said, all three a'us and the Dogs and that Little o'One
Eyed Bear too went over there to say Hidy. Hidy I said, Papa said, we been

a'Missing yall. Oh and then here come a'Bunch of em over to say Hidy back and we scratched they Ears and petted they Cheeks and Annie even give two or three of em a'Kiss and they Kissed her back and nuzzled her Face cause she was the main one Doctored em when we was all back there in The Narrows. They like Old Friends ain't they she said. And then, Papa said, a'couple of em run after o'Fritz and Possum and that Little o'One Eyed Bear like they was trying to chase em off but really they was just Playing cause they was Old Friends too. But then he said I looked round and they was some Horses a'licking on places where other Horses been Hurt and they was other Horses making sure ever body could stay up on they own Feet even if they was Hurting from some Mistreatment or other. But they was one Horse over there down on the Ground with a Bullet in him couldn't hardly breathe and was just a'Coughing and a'Coughing and them other Horses was over there trying to get him up but No they couldn't do it. Then here in a minute, he said, he wadn't Coughing no more And then he wadn't Breathing no more neither, Papa said, and we knowed he was Gone for ever too. That makes me Sad, Annie said. I know it, Papa said, me too. Then Fritz and o'Possum and that Little o'One Eyed Bear went to Crying bout it too cause they wadn't Nothing they could do bout it neither.

THEN NEXT MORNING RIGHT AT SUN UP, Papa said, o'Firefoot of a sudden Screamed and come a'Running through the Creek like a'Wild Panther and then ever other Horse went to Running too. Oh and then, he said, Guns was being Shot off ever wheres and Horses falling Dead or Hurt right and left and o'Calley hollered Ambush Ambush Run Run Run god dam Run and Oh me and Annie jumped up on o'Sister and Oh Yes Sir we did Run Run Run and so did Fritz and o'Possum and that Little o'One Eyed Bear and wadn't no body who wadn't Running cause now Sheriff Pugh and his Men come a'Running out the Night trying to Shoot us Dead Dead Dead and all them Horses too ever one. Oh and then we caught up to all them Other Horses and was Running way back there in the Back but then we seen Johnny and that Big White Horse and o'Firefoot all three go a'Running right through the middle a'the Horses to make a Road for us to Run through the middle and after we Run through it,

Papa said, why them Horses closed up that Road back behind us like some body slammed the Gate Shut so couldn't Sheriff Pugh and his Men even see us to Shoot at no more. Oh it saved our Life, he said, but they was Horses a'Falling and a'Flipping over Dead just bout ever wheres you Looked but we kep a'Running Running Running follering o'Johnny and that Big White Horse ever which way they went, he said, Then here in bout I Don't Know How Long o'Sheriff Pugh and all them Men started getting tired a'chasing us and went to falling behind and we Run on a'head Best we could even if we was all Tired Out too. But what saved our Life was that Big White Horse knowed a'Hiding Place down in this Canyon you could hide out in and keep you self safe. And not only that, Papa said, but they was a Spring down in there running Fresh and Cool. We got lots and lots a'Horses to Doctor, Annie said, and me and o'Calley jumped to the Job right a'long with Annie and it wadn't but another minute or two and we was all three a'Crying at how Bad off most all a'these Horses was and some of em wadn't never gonna get no Better neither. Then, he said, a'Bunch a'them other Horses went to Crying bout it too til you thought you was gonna go Loonie from it.

*B*OUT DARK WHEN WE WAS STILL DOCTORING HORSES, Papa said, o'Johnny and the Big White Horse put out a'bunch a'other Horses to keep Watch all a'long the top a'the Canyon in case o'Sheriff Pugh and his Men tried to come a'Sneaking up on us again. You'd think that Big White Horse was Genral Houston or some body wouldn't you, Papa said, the way he's always thinking a'ever thing. I don't know much as you know bout o'Genral Houston, Annie said, but Yes Sir I reckon thats True if you ask me. And then, he said, when the Sun went all the way down Why more Horses went to Dying and Oh they was such Moaning and a'Crying from the other Ones still a'Live you wanted to put some Mud in your Ears not to hear it. That's the kind a'sound Breaks your Poor o'Heart then Stomps on it ain't it, Calley said, I never heared no Worse in my Life. Me neither, Papa said, and Annie said No Sir not me neither Not in all my Whole Life. But they wadn't no Help for it, Papa said, and we just kep a'Doctoring on em til you couldn't hardly see you Hand in front a'you Face no more it was so Dark. But all this Time, he said, o'Johnny was a'going In and Out a'them Dying Horses and

Guns was being Shot off ever wheres and
Horses falling Dead or Hurt right and left . . .

giving each one a'Pet and some time just when they was a'closing they Eyes for the Last Time he'd give em a'Whisper in they Ear and a Kiss on they Cheek. You reckon o'Johnny knows what he's a'doing, Annie said. I don't know does he or not, Calley said, but I reckon his Heart does cause that's where it's all coming from in the First Place ain't it. I wish we could talk back and forth with him, Papa said. I'd like to tell him he been a Good Friend to all these Mistreated Horses here you know it. Well and to us too, Annie said. He's almost like a Brother ain't he. Oh and when Annie said that, Papa said, why o'Johnny looked over and give us a Smile. You know, Annie said, I never know if he's Smiling bout some thing in particular or just Smiling cause he don't Know no Better. Well either way, Calley said, he's a Smiler ain't he and you can't hardly be round him without you a'Smiling right a'long with him ain't that Right. And course, Papa said, me and Annie went to Smiling too cause Smiling is always Catching ain't it.

*M*E AND ANNIE WAS MARRIED NOW, Papa said, so couldn't no body say nothing bout it when we layed down together out there tween the Horses and looked up at all the Shiney Stars and then one went a'Shooting cross the Sky with they Red Hot Tail on Fire. You gotta make a'Wish, Annie said, and I said I already got my wish Annie my Wish is you and Oh she give me a Squeeze and a Kiss on my Face for that. You just some o'Romantic ain't you she said and I said I reckon I am when it comes to you Annie and she said See that's what I mean Mister and then we went on talking Back and Forth like that a good long while, Papa said, cause we was so in Love and was so Glad to be together in this Life even if we was all in a Fix right now and didn't have no Idea how we was ever gonna get out a'it. You reckon they send People to Hell for Murdering Horses, Annie said. They would if I had anything to say bout it, Papa said, But from what I know they the One sends they own Self down there to set on that Flat Rock when they done some thing Bad up here. Where'd you get this News any how, Annie said, I never heared a'no such thing like it. I'll tell you some other Time, Papa said, I'm busy Hugging my Wife now and Looking up at the Stars and don't wanna talk bout nothing else. Oh and then, he said, we heared o'Calley's spur go Ching e Ching e ChingChingChing over there in the Night some wheres and knowed he was a'wishing he was a'holding his Dead Sweet Heart in his arms too. He ain't never gonna get over Pela Rosa is he, Annie said, and I said No Ma'am he ain't never. Then, he said, we looked up a'the Top a'the Canyon and seen o'Johnny a'setting there on the Big White Horse with all them Stars a'twinkling like Lightning Bugs all over the Sky behind em. You think o'Johnny ever gonna find him a Sweet Heart like ever body else Annie said. Well I think he already got him one ain't he, Papa said. What, Annie said, you ain't talking bout that Big White Horse are you. Well I might be, Papa said, I don't know why not. No I don't Know why not neither Annie said and then he said we give each other a Hug cause a'all this Talk bout Sweet Hearts.

ME AND ANNIE WOKE UP next morning, Papa said, with o'Fritz and Possum and that Little o'One Eyed Bear a'giving us a Push with they Feet to Wake Up and Look and we looked, he said, and what we seen was o'Johnny and that Big White Horse and Firefoot a'going up the side a'the Canyon with all them other Horses a'follering long behind quiet as a'little Mouse. Next thing o'Calley was bended down over us. They want ever body to leave now don't they he said. So, Papa said, we got behind all them Horses and went on up and out the Canyon too and then went a'Sneaking out a'cross the Prairie. What's going on here, Annie said. I think the Big White Horse knows they's some body coming to get us, Calley said, and he wants us to get on a'Way from here fore they do far as I can tell. And then, Papa said, the Big White Horse and o'Firefoot and all them other Horses and us too started a'Trotting and Oh then we all went to Galloping cross the Country Side cause of a sudden here come Sheriff Pugh on his Black Horse and a'Bunch a'his Men a'Swarming down the Hill a'Shooting they guns off at us and they wadn't nothing to do, Papa said, but Run Run Run like we done before and Oh we did Run he said and after bout a Year they started falling back behind us a'gain like before and Oh it was so Good to see that and a big Grin almost come on my Face but No then here come a'Bunch a'other Men down a'nother Hill on Fresh Horses to take over from the First Bunch and Oh now it was us getting more Tireder'n they was. They chasing us in Relays, Calley hollered. Run Run Run.

And Oh we did Run, Papa said, but then of a sudden o'Johnny and the Big White Horse turned round in a big cloud a'Dust and went a'Charging back at Sheriff Pugh and them other Men and then so did o'Firefoot too and not only him but now o'Calley pulled his Pistola and charged back with em fast as he could but they was so much Dust a'flying you couldn't hardly tell what was a'going on cept ever body was Shooting they Guns off at ever body else and Oh then, he said, Oh then I seen o'Johnny grab at his Heart and go a'Falling off the Big White Horse like he been Shot Dead by his own Brother.

O'CALLEY DUCKED ALL THEM BULLETS and come a'Running on back to us, Papa said. Sheriff Pugh just Shot and Killed his own Little Brother Johnny, he said, even if he didn't even know who he was a'Shooting at til it was too Late. And Oh, Papa said, now we seen o'Sheriff Pugh a'holding his Dead Brother Johnny tight in his arms and just a'Crying and a'Hollering up to the Sky to tell God how Mad he was bout it. He killed poor o'Johnny, Annie said, then started Crying bout it too, Papa said, and so did I and that goes for Calley and Fritz and o'Possum and that Little o'One Eyed Bear too. We was all Crying, he said, We was all Crying and just couldn't Stop it. O'Johnny didn't talk much but he was our Friend wadn't he, Annie said. We didn't never have no Better. Then of a sudden Sheriff Pugh went to Shooting at us from way off out yonder and Hollered You the One caused this god dam you Calley Pearsall you the One and I'm gonna Hang you by your god dam Neck for it til you Dead Dead Dead and then, Papa said, o'Sheriff Pugh climbed up on his Black Horse and them other Men hefted his Dead Brother Johnny up to him and he put his Arms round him and rode on off, his Men a'follering long behind but No they wadn't Crying bout it like he was. He didn't know it was his Little Brother Johnny a'riding on that Big Ghost Horse did he, Annie said. No he didn't, Papa said. Well I reckon he knows it now don't he, Calley said. I reckon he just Shot and Killed the Proof a'that his self. And he ain't never gonna get over it neither, he said.

THEY WADN'T SO MANY HORSES ALIVE NOW
as they was before, Papa said, But what they was left went to follering
o'Johnny there in his Big Brother's Arms. And so did the Big White Horse
and o'Firefoot too, he said, but they all stayed a'good Ways back so they
wouldn't get Kilt they self. All them Horses Loved o'Johnny didn't they, Annie said. Well o'Johnny was they Friend, Calley said, it was almost like he
was one of em his self wadn't it. If I was the one putting his Name on the
Grave Stone I believe I'd just say Johnny Horse. Johnny Horse, Annie said.
Yes Ma'am Johnny Horse and nothing else, Calley said. Well I reckon that
Says bout ever thing they is to Say bout o'Johnny ain't it, Papa said. Well
we could say we Loved him too, Annie said. We could say that. Yes we could
and we'd mean it ever Word wouldn't we, Papa said, and his Brother Simon
could say it too even if he's the one Shot and Killed him in the First Place.
Yes Sir, but he Blames me for it, Calley said. And I reckon he's gonna Blame
all them Horses for it too ain't he. Ain't them or us neither one near outta
the Woods yet if you ask me he said. We gotta keep pushing what we got left
a'the Horses on West, Annie said. Less that Big White Horse got a'different
Idea bout it, Calley said, cause them Horses listen to him lot moren they
gonna listen to us. He's they Big Chief ain't he, Papa said. I'm not xactly sure
What he is, Calley said, but I never seen no Horses a'Standing up for They
self the Way these Horses been a'doing here lately have you. If theys a'Horse
World I reckon that Big White Horse is the One runs it, he said. Yes Sir and
it cost a'Bunch of em they Life too didn't it, Annie said. If you don't like the
Music you a'Dancing to Why they's always some body gonna come a'long
and Change the Tune no matter what the Cost, Calley said. You ever heared
that Annie. I did hear it one time, Annie said, but I didn't have no Idea it was
gonna make me so Sad til just now Mister Pearsall.

OH WE LOOKED AND WE LOOKED AND WE LOOKED,
Papa said, but No them Horses wadn't No Wheres to be Seen. They's some
thing wrong here, Annie said, they wouldn't a'just run off and left us would
they. No not less some body Tricked em in to it they wouldn't, Calley said.
So we rode over the Hill to see what we could see on the other side, Papa
said, and Oh way off out yonder we seen bout a'hunderd a'the Sheriff's Men

a'Rounding up those horses and Herding em on off Cross the Country to-ward San Antoneya. It's them Relay Men doubled back to catch em, Calley said, and it was the Horses Love for poor o'Dead Johnny turned out to be the Bait to do it with. What're we gonna do, Annie said. They's so many of em. Ain't nothing we can do, Calley said, not Now any how. But, he said, they gonna have to keep em all in one Place oncet they get em to San Antoneya and by god we'll just sure as Hell do some thing bout it then. You don't figgur they setting a Trap to catch us in too do you, Papa said. Yes Sir they might be, Calley said, and it's our Job not to Fall in it if they do Mister. Oh and then we seen some a'Sheriff Pugh's Men had Ropes tied all over the Big White Horse and o'Firefoot both and was a'Whupping em to make em Go cause they didn't want to. Them SonsaBitches, Calley said, ever god dam one of em to go beating a'Horse like that. I'd tell em too, Annie said, right to they Face if I was down there. I would too, Papa said, and Calley said And me right there a'long side the Both a'you. But they wadn't nothing we could do bout it from way back there where we was, Papa said, so we just kep a'follering with our Heads down so they wouldn't see us. This is Pretty Country we a'going through here ain't it, Annie said, I just wish they wadn't so much Trouble in it for Horses. And for us too I reckon, o'Calley said.

*W*E FOLLERED EM BOUT ALL THE WAY to San Antoneya, Papa said, but of a Sudden o'Calley said Let's us just Hold Up here a minute and then he went to picking Flowers. Oh they was Butter Cups and Blue Bonnets and Fire Wheels and Yeller Daseys and Indian Blankets, Papa said, and all them other Flowers my Momma used to go round naming for me when I was still just a'Little Boy. He's picking em for Pela Rosa ain't he Annie said and I knowed that was True, Papa said, so we rode long behind til we got over to that Place where we buried his Sweet Heart Pela Rosa after o'Sheriff Pugh went and Killed her Dead that Day even if it was by Accident. Oh and then, he said, Fritz and o'Possum and that Little Bear went over there to be Friends with him and o'Calley took his John B off and layed them Flowers down on her Grave like they was his own Tears. Oh that's Sad ain't it Annie said and I said Yes Annie Sad Sad Sad but the

He's picking em for Pela Rosa ain't he Annie said
and I knowed that was True, Papa said . . .

Thing bout it was he wadn't Crying bout it and that bout Scared me out my Pants cause a'what o'Calley used to say. What ever you a'Looking for in Your Life, he used to say, Is out there some wheres in the World a'Looking for you too. But we had to get on to San Antoneya quick's we could, Papa said, and I didn't have no more Time to Worry bout him a'Looking for a way to be over there on the Other Side with his Sweet Heart.

*W*E SNEAKED IN TO SAN ANTONEYA in Secret, Papa said, and seen o'Sheriff Pugh and his Men a'Running all them Horses down the Street pass the Alamo and Oh, he said, they was People a'coming from ever which Direction to Watch em go by. But you could tell some of em was Mad bout what they was seeing cause they loved Horses and Animals and didn't want nothing Bad to ever happen to em But they was Others who was Glad of it cause they reckoned all these Horses here is Horse Theifs they self and they didn't hold no Truck for Theifs a'any kind Man or Beast. Then they Run em on pass the Alamo, Papa said, and Oh that Hanging Stand they made to Hang o'Calley from was still out there in the Street just a'waiting for his Neck to go in and maybe mine too I reckon cause I was the one helped o'Calley get a'way in the First Place and o'Sheriff Pugh wadn't likely to just let it go. But just to be sure, he said, I ducked my John B down so couldn't no body see my Face when we went a'riding by and Annie did hers too just in case but o'Calley just throwed his Shoulders back like he didn't have a'Care in the World and didn't give no Caution was any body a'Looking at him or not.

Oh them poor Horses was so Tired and Wore Out from all they Running and being Chased and being Shot at, Papa said, why they could just barely get on down the Street but the Sheriff's Men kep a'giving em Pops with they Quirts and Slaps with they Ropes and didn't never stop Hollering at em to Git Git Git and then after bout a Year and six Days they run em on in the Pen over there on Military Plaza and closed the Big Gate to Lock em in but didn't give em no Water to Drink for they Thirst. Then, he said, here come this little Mexkin Boy with a'Bucket a'Water to give em a'Drink but one a'the Sheriff's Men went over there and knocked it out his Hand then just to be Mean laughed bout it and give that Little Fella a'Good Hard Kick in his Pants and run him on back out the Pen where he come from. I'm gonna remember that Sorry Son of a Bitch when it comes Bill Paying Time, Calley said, and me and Annie both said Me Too Me Too.

*B*OUT DARK, Papa said, we sneaked in the Back Door at Senyora Garza's Place and Oh we was Glad to see her and she was Glad to see us too. I been Worryed sick bout yall, she said, I didn't have no Idea was yall a'Live or Dead. We been trying to keep Sheriff Pugh from Murdering Horses, Calley said. It ain't easy. I know it, Senyora Garza said, and now he got that Big Bunch of em in the Pen over there at Military Plaza. What you reckon he's gonna do with em, Annie said. I know xactly what he's gonna do with em, Calley said. He's gonna Xecute em sames he would any other Horse Theif. And you too Senyor Pearsall if he ever catches you, Senyora Garza said. Xecute em, Papa said. Xecute em. You don't mean he's gonna Hang em do you, Annie said. You don't mean that. Probably Shoot em in the Pen with ever body a'Watching, Senyora Garza said, but I don't know. Sheriff Pugh takes him a Drink in here ever now and a'gain, she said, but he don't never confide in me. For a'minute, Papa said, o'Calley couldn't even Talk he was so scared for o'Firefoot and the Big White Horse and all them other Mistreated Horses too. And so was Fritz and o'Possum and that Little o'One Eyed Bear a'setting there at the Table with us. Well we ain't gonna let that happen by god, Calley said, I don't care What it takes. You gonna need some Help, Senyora Garza said. I got some Friends. They'd be risking they Life for a'Bunch a'Horses, Calley said, you'd have to tell em that so they know What they a'getting in to here. These Friends I'm talking bout ain't scared to Die, she said, or they wouldn't be a'living here in Texas in the First Place. You must be talking bout some Mexkins you know then huh Calley said and Senyora Garza said Si Senyor, Family. Well it don't surprise me, Calley said.

SENYORA GARZA'S LITTLE BROTHER

was named Ponchito, Papa said, cause he wadn't no moren bout eight years old and not only that, he said, but we already knowed him cause he was the One tryed to give them Horses a'Drink a'Water out his little Bucket down there at the Pen fore the Sheriff's Man kicked him in the Pants and run him off. The other one, Papa said, was her o'Uncle Luis who was borned in Mexico but crossed over the River to here when he was still just a'little Bean his self and, Senyora Garza said, he been Here ever since even if he wanted to go back Home same Day he waded over. Oh and then here come a'nother Five Six Mexkins, Papa said, and a'nother Two Three after that. And not only them, he said, but now here come Four Five Germans right long behind carrying they Big German Bird Guns. Them Germans must a'married in to the Family huh, Calley said, but Senyora Garza said No Senyor they just don't want no Body round here a'hurting Horses. Then o'Calley looked over at me and Annie and said Theys more Germans come over on the Boat to San Antoneya than they ever was Mexkins waded cross the River to get here Did you know that. No Sir, Papa said, this is the First I ever heared of it. Just Pay a'tention and you'll learn some thing New ever day, Calley said, Ain't that Right Annie. He Knows Plenty, Annie said, then give him a'Look and said He don't have to know ever thing. O'Calley give up on her then, Papa said, and looked over at all them Others. Yall know what we talking bout doing here don't you, Calley said. I wouldn't want it to be no Surprise to no body when they go to Shooting at us. We gonna Steal them Horses down there in the Pen, Luis said. Ain't that Right. No we're gonna set em Free, Annie said, they the ones been doing all the Horse Stealing round here. They was so Thirsty I tryed to give em a'Drink a'Water Ponchito said. That was a Brave Thing to do I'm glad to know you Amigo, Calley said, then give him a Nod and a'little Knock on his Head. I'm glad to know you too, Papa said. We all are, Annie said, and give him a'nother little Knock on his Head to show him we meant it ever Word. Gracias, Ponchito said, and then Luis reached over and give him a Knock on his head too I reckon just cause ever body else been a'doing it, Papa said. How you going to do this, Senyora Garza said. I don't know yet, Calley said. We gonna have to set and think bout it a'minute. They gonna be Watching if you ask me, Annie said. Yes Ma'am, Calley said. And they gonna have they Guns out too ain't they, Papa said. Yes Sir Mister, Calley said, that is xactly right. And they gonna Shoot you with em too you know it, Senyora Garza said. Nein, I don't like this so much, one of the Germans said. I wouldn't want you doing nothing you don't wanna do Mister, Calley said. This is a'Scarey Busness we got here. No I vanna save them Horses, the German said, I just don't like it ven some body starts Shooting at me for doing it. I didn't like it neither, Papa said, but I didn't Say Nothing cause they wadn't Nothing to Say if we was gonna go on and do it any how and I knowed we was cause we wadn't never gonna Go Back on our Word to save them Horses if we could.

SENYORA GARZA COOKED UP A'POT A'BEANS, Papa said, and we was setting there at the Table in her Place getting ready to eat em when here come two Men putting the News out they was gonna bury Poor o'Johnny in the Grave Yard tomorra and his brother Sheriff Simon Pugh wanted ever body in Town to go out there and say Goodbye. Then after they left Calley said I didn't know How we was gonna save all them Horses but by god I do now. And When too he said. O'Johnny'd like us Saving em same time they a'burying him wouldn't he. I don't know how any body'd ever come up with a better Good Bye to o'Johnny'n that do you, Papa said. We ain't done it yet Mister, Calley said. I wouldn't go to Counting my Chickens fore they Hatch. I wouldn't neither, Annie said, you might wind up with just a'Handful a'Feathers. Then, Papa said, Calley looked over there at Ponchito and said Ponchito you reckon you could sneak in that Pen tomorra Morning with out no body a'seeing you and unlatch the Gate for us and Ponchito said Si Senyor no Problema I can do it. So early next Morning, he said, we found us a'Hiding Place behind a'Building to watch from when here come o'Sheriff Pugh and his Men a'walking down the Street with o'Johnny dead in his Box and ever body in Town out there in the Street a'Crying cause o'Johnny become one a'they very own over the years and now they was Sorry to see him go. And then, Papa said, when they passed on by on they way out to the Grave Yard Ponchito run over there and sneaked the Gate open and now us and the Mexkins and the Germans all run over there in the Pen to tell all them Horses they was Free to Go now but Oh, he said, Turned out they wadn't just Horses in the Pen but was a'Bunch a'the Sheriff's Men all Ducked down and Hiding tween em with they Guns out to Shoot us if we didn't Stop and put our Hands Up in the Air Right this god dam minute like they told us to do. And then, Papa said, Why here come o'Sheriff Pugh back from down the Street cause he hadn't gone to the Grave Yard to bury his Little Brother like he said he was gonna do but just gone down the Street a little ways til he had us in his Trap and now here he was back a'gain. Well you in a Fix now ain't you Mister he said and give o'Calley a'Mean Hit with his Pistol but Oh when he did, Papa said, why here come Firefoot a'Baring his Teeth and a'Screaming from out the Horses and give the Sheriff a hit back with his Chest that put him to the Ground and then, he said, o'Firefoot reared up on his hind Feet to Stomp him Dead in the Ground but Calley jumped out there in front a'him and Hollered No Firefoot No No No but it was too late and o'Firefoot Stomped at o'Sheriff Pugh any how but he rolled out the way just in Time and give poor o'Firefoot Three Bullets straight in his Heart ONE TWO THREE and o'Firefoot went down Dead right there in front a'the Best Friend he ever did have in his Life.

OH AND THEN, Papa said, o'Calley went to Screaming and Hollering like a Crazy Man and went after Sheriff Pugh with just his Bare Hands to Kill him if he could but the Sheriff come round with his Pistol and give him two quick Bullets right there in his Belly BOOM BOOM and o'Calley went down like Some-body dropped a'Anvil on him. Oh, he said, Oh and then Me and Annie let go a'Holler and went at o'Sheriff Pugh ourself for what he just done to our Friend and Firefoot and so did Fritz and o'Possum and that Little o'One Eyed Bear too but the Sheriff's Men come a'Running over there and Whupped us back with they Pistols and they Fists til we was a'Spitting and Blowing Blood ever which way. Oh and all this Whole Time they was a'Whomping on us, Papa said, they was some Others still out there a'Shooting Horses and Mexkins and Germans and they just wadn't no Quit in em when it come to Murder. Then, he said, they went to grabbing us to throw us in the Jail House and poor o'Calley just barely a'Breathing. But right then, Papa said, here come this big Commotion from up the Street and what it was he said Was all them Men Women and Little Chilren been out there at the Grave Yard a'Burying o'Johnny but now here they was a'coming back but Oh listen

. . . o'Calley went to Screaming and Hollering like a Crazy Man and went after Sheriff Pugh with just his Bare Hands to Kill him if he could but the Sheriff come round with his Pistol and give him two quick Bullets right there in his Belly BOOM BOOM . . .

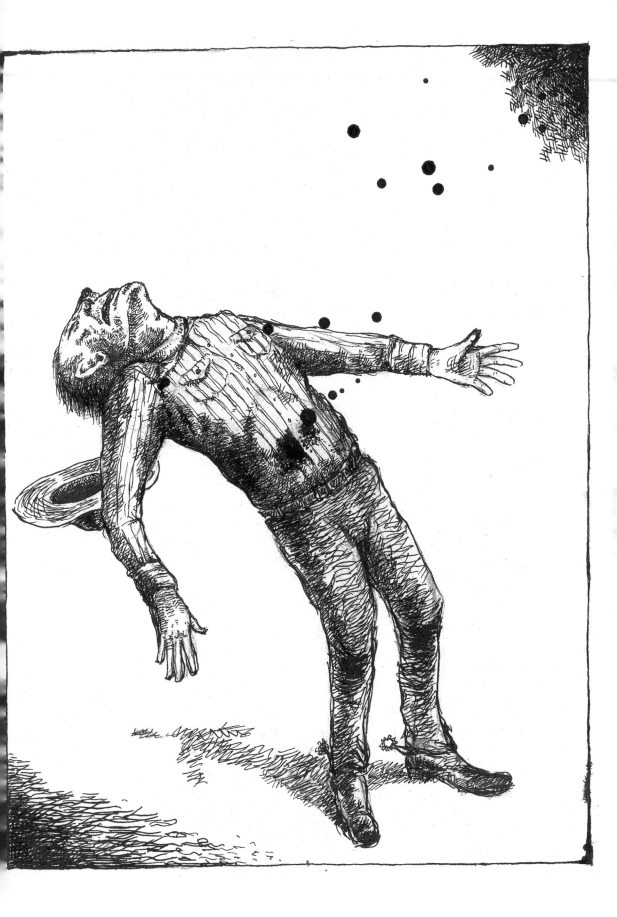

here, Papa said, they wadn't none of em Happy bout Seeing all these Dead Horses we got here and all these Dead Mexkins and Dead Germans long with em. Oh and then here come this big o'German Woman name a'Erna I believe it was just went a'Hollering when she seen her dead Husband Otto a'laying out there next to a'couple a'Dead Mexkins. OH OTTO she Hollered. OTTO OTTO OTTO and then some Mexkin Woman down the Street went to Hollering PABLO PABLO PABLO cause she just seen her Husband Dead too next to some German and couldn't get over it. Oh and they was People just a'Crying and a'Carrying on bout all these Dead Horses we got here too and o'Sheriff Pugh and his Men cocked they Pistols and went over there to tell em Just Shut Up bout it cause All these Dead Horses was Horse Theifs too and was gonna get Xecuted one way or the other any how but one Man went over there and grabbed up o'Sheriff Pugh by his Shirt and said Well by God my Nellie wadn't no Horse Theif and o'Sheriff Pugh knocked that Man's Hand off his Shirt with his Pistol and said Well your o'Nellie run with Horse Theifs it's the same god dam thing ain't it. And Oh, he said, People started a'coming from all up and down the Street just a'Shaking they Fists at o'Sheriff Pugh and his Men for what all they done here. And then of a Sudden, Papa said, Why here come Senyora Garza and Little Ponchito a'sneaking up with this Donkey Cart they had and got us on down the Street and Out a'town in it fore any more Harm come to us.

ME AND ANNIE EACH TOOK HOLD A' O'CALLEY'S HANDS to comfort him if we could, Papa said, but they was Bumps ever step a'the Way and it Hurt him some thing Awful ever one of em. He ain't gonna Die is he, Annie said. I don't want him to Die. But I didn't say nothing, Papa said, cause I was fraid I'd start crying if I did so I squeezed o'Calley's Hand in sted and give him a'little Tickle in his Ribs to see if his Funny Bone was still working but No, he said, o'Calley didn't give nothing back. I think he's a'sleeping I said, Papa said. That's good ain't it, Annie said. He could use him some Rest after all he been through today I reckon. Yes Ma'am I reckon so I said then turned my Head like I was looking for Indians or some thing so she wouldn't see the Tears a'coming up in my Eyes.

Then long bout Mid Night we come to this little Mud House out there in the Country some wheres and all these Mexkins come out to help carry o'Calley back in and put him on the Bed. Ay Ay Ay one of em said He don't look so good to me. I know it, Senorya Garza said, but we got to Save him if we can you know it. So, Papa said, they went to washing out his Bullet Holes and Praying and Making Hand signs over him to help Save him but No didn't look like nothing was working cause o'Calley just layed there like a Knot on a Log and didn't let out a Peep. It's not so Good, Senyora Garza said. He ain't gonna Die is he, Annie said. I don't know, Senyora Garza said, we can't do no more for him now cep Pray so, Papa said, they all reached out and put they Hands on Him and Oh just went to Praying Praying Praying but couldn't me or Annie neither one understand a'Lick a'what they was a'Praying cause we didn't speak they Language. And then Annie said Don't make no Difference we speak they Language or not They ain't a'talking to us any how are they. Oh and then Papa said we took a'Hold'a o'Calley's Hands a'gain and went to Praying our self and now here come the Creatures to push up close a'gainst him and Cry too. This is a Bad Time we got here Annie I said, Papa said, and Annie said Yes it is Yes it is. But they wadn't no Help for it, he said, and all we could do was just set there Praying like that and a'holding his Hand so he'd know he wadn't all a'Lone in the World and wadn't never gonna be long as we was there. And then, Papa said, I reckon I closed my Eyes.

H AND THEN, Papa said, Here come o'Jeffey in my Dream with all them Dead Horses just a'Shimmering all a'round her. And then next, he said, Here come some o'Shimmery Man a'walking out from all them Shimmery Horses and I thought Yes Sir I know this Man don't I but No Sir couldn't place Him but I give him a Smile any how and then he give me a Smile back and rolled his Eyes all round like some o'Loonie and Oh, Papa said, Oh right then I knowed Why this is o'Johnny his self ain't it but he been all Restored ain't he cause now he got him some Regular Size Arms and some Regular Size Feet and is a Regular Size Man in ever way they is to be Regular. Johnny this is You ain't it, I said, Yes Sir this is you sure nough ain't it. You a Whole New Man now

ain't you I said. But o'Jeffey said No this ain't a whole New Johnny we got here. This is the Same o'Johnny they always been. He just Boogered his self up this time round to be that Poor o'Loonie you talking bout so when People seen him they'd have to reach way down deep inside they own Heart to find the Best Person they ever was in there and be Nice to him cause being Nice to Creatures and o'Loonies is one a'the Bestus Ways they is or Was or ever Will Be to Keep from having to go down there and Set on that Flat Rock til Kingdom Come. Ain't that Right Hon, she said, then reached over and give o'Johnny a Pet on his Cheek and a Scruff on his Head. That was the Whole Reason he come down here this Time in the First Place. To help each one a'us to find our Best Self. It was his Gift to the Rest a'us, she said, wadn't it Hon and then Johnny give me a Look like he been a Bad Little Boy and said Sorry for all the Trouble and I said No it wadn't no Trouble Johnny and he said Well Thank You for all the Help any how I love you very much then he give me a Hug and then somebody else Squeezed my Hand but I looked down and seen No they wadn't No Body there to be a'squeezing my Hand like that and Oh I come on Up and Out a'my Dream like Some Body just chunked a'Tub a'Wet Rattle Snakes on me cause I knowed it was o'Calley Pearsall his self a'Squeezing my Hand like that cause he wanted to say Adios Amigo Adios fore it was too Late.

YOU AIN'T DEAD

yet are you Calley I said, Papa said and o'Calley's Eyes come open to a'little narrow crack. Oh. Oh Now I can see all them Shimmery People you been talking bout all this Time he said. Look close, Papa said, I reckon a'Bunch of em is People you already know from your Life. He started Smiling then and his Eyes went to jumping round Here and There Here and There like he was seeing somebody or other he knowed ever wheres he looked Then he reached his Hand out to One of em in particular and come up on his Elbow just a'Smiling. Well ain't you the Pretty One, he said. Oh it bout made me Cry to see my o'Amigo so Happy. It's your Sweet Heart Pela Rosa ain't it I said. No, o'Calley said. It's my Little Dog the Tonks stole out from under the Porch that night and et for their suppers. Then he patted the Bed for his Little Dog to jump up on there next to him and Died.

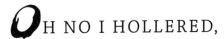

OH NO I HOLLERED, Papa said. OH NO OH NO OH NO. But wadn't no use, he said, o'Calley was Gone from this World forever. Gone Gone Gone. Oh and then that awful Copper Taste come up in my mouth like in a Big Flood at what o'Sheriff Pugh done to my Friend. You thinking Bad Things there ain't you, Annie said, and I said I reckon I'm thinking the only Thing I got to Think Annie. I ain't able to think no other. Then, Papa said, I grabbed Calley's Big o'Pistola up off the Bed and give the cylindar a'Couple a'Whirls to make sure they was plenty a'Bullets in it for when I was gonna need em. You bout to take you a'Ride on the Devil's Fork there ain't you Mister, Annie said and I said I reckon I'm already on it Annie then stuck Calley's o'Pistola way down deep in my Pants to where I wouldn't Lose it on my Ride back to San Antoneya for my Revenge. We gonna need to give him a Good Bath and Clean him up for when We take him Home, Senyora Garza said, Where is that any way. I don't know that he had one, Papa said, but I reckon he'd like it just fine to be over there in the Choats Grave Yard with ever body else already Gone. I think he'd like it we go get Pela Rosa and take her over there with him, Annie said, Don't you reckon. That's a'good Idea, Papa said. You always Thinking ain't you Annie. It's You I'm thinking bout, Annie said, But I know I can't talk Good Sense in you. You just too Hard Headed and Stubborn for that. Oh and then here come Senyora Garza and all them other Mexkin Ladies with they Soap and Water and started giving o'Calley a Bath from Head to Toe then Combed his hair back with a'little Part right down the Middle. I wish we had a Clean Shirt to put on him, Annie said. Why that'd make him feel Better don't you reckon. No he's Happy long as he got his John B over his Chest, Papa said, I wouldn't worry bout it. Then Senyora Garza come over with a'Silver Locket had that Pitchur a'him and me in it that was made over there in the Joske Brother Store that time and I reckon he been a'wearing it in Secret over his Heart ever since. You might want this for yourself she said but I showed her the One I kep in my Pocket just like it, Papa said, and told her she better go on and put that One back round o'Calley's Neck where she found it. I don't think he'd wanna part with it no moren I would mine I said, then turned and wiped a Tear from off my Face.

131

I SADDLED O'SISTER UP,

Papa said, then went back in the House to say Adios to Ever Body. I guess they just ain't no Talking you out a'this is they, Annie said, and I said No I'm Sorry they ain't Annie and give the Creatures each one a'little Pet but o'Fritz bared his Teeth and ducked my Pet cause he was Mad at me for Going and not taking him with me. No Fritz you got to Stay with Annie, Papa said, I ain't got time to fool with you today but, he said, o'Fritz went to Licking on his Hiney like he didn't never care nothing bout Going any how. He's gonna do that all Day long if you don't take him with you Annie said. Course I knowed he was probably gonna do that all Day long any how, Papa said, but I said Okay Fritz you can Come but you got to Mine and Behave you self. Then o'Fritz give me a Look and went Heh Heh Heh. You wanna say Good Bye to Mister Pearsall fore you leave don't you Annie said. Course I knowed that wadn't really o'Calley a'laying there with his Hair Parted down the Middle like that but was really just the Shell he shucked when o'Sheriff Pugh put two Bullets in it so it couldn't go no more. Adios o'Amigo I said and Thumbed my John B back like him and me used to do when we was a'saying See You Later Mister.

Annie follered me and Fritz out to where o'Sister was Waiting. You ain't gonna stay mad at me for Going are you Annie I said and Annie said Well I might if you don't come back but then, Papa said, she give me a Sweet Kiss Good Bye to let me know she was only just Joking bout it and a'way we did go but I didn't look back cause it was too Hard and I Knowed I might never get over it.

IT'S ONE THING TO JUST GO A'RIDING

out cross the Country with a'Little Dog in your Lap, Papa said, but it's a whole nother Thing you got a big o'Pistola stuck down your Pants like I did. Why of a sudden he said I was a'lot Biggern I ever been in my Regular Life and started to Wishing I'd been in the Fray with o'Sammy Houston and his Boys to show ever body how Mean and Dangerous I was. Course, Papa said, I knowed that was Calley's Big o'Pistola doing most a'the Talking and I was gonna have to find some Spunk a'my own when the Time come to Deal with o'Sheriff Simon Pugh. But then, he said, this big o'Block a'Froze Ice come a'Creeping up my Back cause What if they wadn't even nough Spunk in me to find in the First Place. So I was just riding long feeling Worried bout my self like that, Papa said, when here in a minute I come up behind this Man and his Wife and they Little Chilren in they Wagon a'going the same Direction I was. Morning the Man said Where you headed. San Antoneya I said. You ever been there. No but Going now for the Hanging same as you I reckon huh, the Man said. No I didn't even know they was a Hanging, Papa said, Who is it they a'Hanging. I don't have no Idea Who just Some body done Some thing Bad I reckon, the Man said. You ever seen a'Hanging. No Sir I said. I seen One one time, the Man said, but it didn't hardly count. Bet it did to the Man was Hanged, the Man's Wife said and give him the Sour Puss. Why didn't it Count, Papa said. Cause it was just some o'Mexkin, the Man said, that's Why. Well I reckon he Counted much as any body else in the World Counted, Papa said. Well your Young and don't know Much do you the Man said. I started to pull my Shirt back and show him the Big o'Pistola I had, Papa said, but No I decided I'd do my own Talking. I know Plenty I said, Papa said, but then couldn't think a'nothing else to say to Back it up. Then the Man said Your o'Daddy never took you to a'Hanging did he huh and I said No Sir he never did. Well the Man said I'm taking mine to give em a Good Lesson bout Right and Wrong course it ain't gonna be much of a'Lesson if it's just some o'Mexkin they a'Hanging is it. Would be to me I said. Same as if it was some o'German or China Man. Oh then his o'Wife give me a little Nod for what I said but was careful her Man didn't see it. Then the Man give me a different Look'n Hers and said Well maybe we'll see you there and I said Well you sure gonna have to Look Hard if you Wanna see me there Mister cause I ain't Planning to go.

*B*OUT A HOUR OR TWO LATER, Papa said, I come up behind these Seven Old Men a'walking down the Road with a Little Round Table and some Chairs on they Back and I knowed just who they was too. Where's all your Black and White Dominoes at I said, Papa said, but they wouldn't hardly even Look up at me. You go on, the Old Black Man said, maybe we'll talk to you later. Oh and then here come that Block a'Froze Ice up my Back again, Papa said, cause they usually just said

You go on now it ain't your Time yet. Yall ain't saying it's my Time coming up here Pretty Quick now are you I said. You ain't saying that. We ain't saying Nothing Mister, the Old Inyin Man said. It just depends Senyor, the Old Mexkin Man said. Yes Sir that's right the Old White Man said, Just all Depends. Just all Depends on what, Papa said. Yall talking in Riddles now ain't you. Just all Depends on you, the Old Inyin Man said. That's all. Yall always been Nice to me before I said, What's making Yall so Mean to me now. We always liked Who you was, the Old Black Man said, We just don't know if We gonna like Who you maybe gonna become here Shortly. Well Who'm I gonna become here Shortly I said. You got to decide that for you self Senyor, the old Mexkin Man said. It ain't No Body's Place to Decide for you. Then they give each other a'Sad Look like they was Worried bout some thing or Other and went on down the Road with they Table and Chairs, Papa said, And then me and o'Fritz went on down the Road too.

THE MORE CLOSE WE GOT TO SAN ANTONEYA, Papa said, the more People they was on the Road a'going there too. Then these Three Men drunk on some thing come a'riding over long side me and one of em said You a'going to the Hanging in San Antoneya too huh. But No, Papa said, I couldn't tell em I was going to San Antoneya to Shoot the Sheriff so I just said No I don't know nothing bout no Hanging Mister. Well, he said, they was this Man Murdered the Sheriff's Little Brother and now the Sheriff's gonna Hang him for it. I knowed a'course he was talking bout o'Calley so I said No Sir I believe that Man you talking bout there already left the Country for good and ain't never coming back. Well, the Next Man said, might not be him but might be o'Sin Nombre the Boy Bandit his self who usted to run with him when they was out Robbing and Shooting People all over the Country. Yeah o'Sin Nombre, the First Man said, He's the One robbed them two Poor Old People that time ain't he. Robbed em and Murdered em both, the other Man said, Then left em out there in the Pasture for the Ants to eat. Wadn't nothing left but they Finger Nails idn't that right, the Third Man said. Just they Finger Nails and the Old Woman's Ring but some body got off with the Ring fore the Family could claim it the way I heared it. Yes Sir, he said, and they was them other Two used to go a'Robbing and a'Murdering with him but o'Sin Nombre got Mad at em one day and tyed em to they own Horse to where they couldn't never get off even to Relieve they self but had to Go on and Go to where ever they Horses wanted to Go and they starved to Death tyed to they Horses like that til they wadn't no more left of em but just Skin and Bones. I seen em like that myself one time the First man said. Just Skin and Bones a'Riding they Horses and o'Sin Nombre a'setting over there on the Hill just a'Laughing bout it. Wadn't never no Sin Nombre in the First Place, Papa said, That's just some o'Story some body round here been telling. Yes Sir Mister Sonny Boy, the First Man said, Well let's just See what you think bout it when o'Sin Nombre steps out from behind a Rock some wheres and feeds you to the Ants like he done them two Old People we was a'talking bout. Then he give me a'Look and bout Swallered his own Tongue, Papa said, and I seen he was one a'them Bad Mean Drunks like my own Daddy usted to be and No Sir I didn't want no part a'him so I just give em a'little Tip a'my John B and went on down the Road with out a'saying a'nother Word.

WE COME TO SAN ANTONEYA

bout Dark, Papa said, and Oh they was already so many People in Town for the Hanging you'd a'thought it was o'Genral Houston's Birthday. They's more People here'n you can shake a'Stick at ain't they Fritz I said and he give his Hiney a'little Lick to say he didn't much care bout it one way or the other. Then, Papa said, I put my Hand on Calley's big o'Pistola and we rode over there to the Jail House so I could shoot o'Sheriff Pugh Dead Dead Dead like I come all this way to do. But, Papa said, they was so many People a'milling round I couldn't even find him no wheres in the Crowd. This ain't the Right Time is it Fritz I said, Maybe we'll just come back and Shoot him when he goes to Hang that Poor Man he's gonna Hang. So me and o'Fritz passed on by and then, Papa said, here we come a'Riding by the Hanging Stand out there in front a'the Alamo and I took my John B off my Head and put it on my Heart like Calley always said do cause the Alamo is really more a'Church'n anything else. Then I seen this Shimmery Man way over yonder in the Crowd Lift his Hat up at me and give me a Wave to say Hidy and I waved back cause I knowed him from the Last Time I was here. He's the

143

one Run off from the Big Fight with the Mexkins here that Day and been so Mad at his self ever since for a'doing it he decided he ain't never gonna Run Off from here ever a'gain til Kingdom Come. You the One run off from the Fight with the Mexkins that Day ain't you I said when we got over there to him. Yes Sir that was me he said but he didn't Look so Mad at his self bout it no more. You Look like you feeling a'lot Better bout it now ain't you I said and he said You know I was just follering what was already there in side me when I run off that Day. Yes Sir, Papa said, and What was that. I just didn't wanna Shoot no Body is What, he said. But they was always some body a'Hollering at me to Go Shoot a Mexkin less you a'Yeller Belly. But No he said I wadn't never no Yeller Belly I was just follering what always been there in side me in the First Place. Oh and then he give me a Happy little Shimmer, Papa said, and I said Well I'm surprised you still here if you got all your Troubles worked out. No I like to Whisper in People's Ear now, he said, like all these Others round here a'doing. And then I looked round and Yes Sir they was Shimmery People a'Whispering in Regular People's Ear just bout ever wheres you looked. I remember them from Last Time I was here, Papa said. They Whispering things in People's Ear them people already Know but just ain't been able to Remember they Know. Ain't that Right, I said. Oh Yes Sir that is Right he said. And that's Why we come here to the Church to do it Cause the People coming here is always hoping to get Answers for Questions they ain't even been able to Ask they self yet. Like You he said. I don't know that I got a Question or not, Papa said. It don't matter, the Shimmery Man said, I got the Answer for you any how. Then, Papa said, he cupped his Hands round my Ear and whispered They ain't really no Devil's Fork in all the World Mister. The only Devil's Fork they is, he said, is the One right there inside you self.

WELL NOW JUST HOLD ON THERE

I said to myself, Papa said, I wanna think bout this a'minute fore I go off and Shoot some body Dead. So I Whistled o'Fritz and Sister over and me and them went on down there to the San Antoneya River and I set down on a'Flat Rock to Think bout it. First Thing I thought was how o'Calley used to say Whatever you a'Looking for in this Life is Some Wheres out there in the World a'Looking for you too and, Papa said, Another thing my o'Amigo used to always say was Almighty God don't go round Choosing ever body's Life for em but just lets ever body Choose it for they self. You Choose he says, Calley said. You Choose and if you wanna really see who you are, he said, just look at What All you Choosed for you self this time round cause didn't no God or No Body else Choose it for you. And another thing o'Calley said one time was If you don't like the Life you Choosed for you self This Time why you can just go and Choose you self a'different one Next Time. Long as you ain't setting on a'Flat Rock down there some wheres, he said, cause you don't never wanna Choose one gonna keep you from Choosing a'Bunch a'other Ones later on. Oh and Then, Papa said, it come to me how much o'Calley been a'missing his Sweet Heart Pela Rosa and how much he wanted to be with her and then of a Sudden why here come o'Sheriff Pugh and helped him do it by Shooting him Dead. And that's xactly what o'Calley was a'Looking for in the First Place wadn't it. Oh and then I looked cross the River and here come Annie and Senyora Garza in that Little Donkey Cart but now they was three Bodies all wrapped up in Blankets in the back long with o'Possum and that Little o'One Eyed Bear. Who all you got there Annie I said and she said Well we got Mister Pearsall and Pela Rosa like we said we was gonna do but we went on and got that o'Panther too so he could be there with Little Missey. They both gonna like that, Papa said, and I did too. I been a'missing you Annie I said. Well it's only been bout the time it takes to drink a glass a'Water she said but I been a'Missing you my self. You ain't Shot No Body yet have you. No Ma'am and I ain't a'gonna, Papa said, They's just too much Trouble goes long with it. Sides that, he said, I don't reckon that's really o'Calley and Pela Rosa and Little Missey's o'Panther there in the Cart any how but just the Shells they was wearing this Time round.

 OH AND THEN, Papa said they was a BIG BOOM come all the way down from up Yonder in front a'the Alamo at the Hanging Stand and then bout Six Seven Hunderd Mexkins went to a'Strumming on they Guitars and I don't have no Idea how many Germans went to Blowing on they Horns like I used to wanna do my self. Oh Lawdy, he said, and then the San Antoneya River started a'Bubbling

and a'Boiling up like they was some body down there under the water built em a'Big Fire. Oh Lawdy Lawdy, Papa said, and then of a'Sudden here come o'Johnny on that Big White Horse just a'Blowing and a'Shimmering up out the Water like they been Shot out a'Cannon and then after them Why here come all them Dead Horses just a'Snorting and a'Blowing and a'Dancing up out the River in a Row. Oh and I seen a'lot of em was them same Mistreated Horses me and Annie and o'Calley Doctored back to Good Health but course they was Murdered by o'Sheriff Pugh and his Boys over there in the Pen just yester Day and just when the Last One come a'Dancing up out the River I heared this little Ching e Ching e ChingChingChing and Oh Lawdy Lawdy Law here come o'Firefoot a'flying up out the Water like his Pants was on Fire and a'setting there on his Back just a'Whooping and a'Laughing and a'Carrying on wadn't nobody in the World but o'Calley Pearsall his self the Best Friend me and o'Firefoot ever did have in our Life and setting there in o'Calley's Lap just a'Laughing and a'Carrying on same as him was his Sweet Heart Pela Rosa and they was all Three just a'Shimmering Shimmering Shimmering Shimmering but, Papa said, if that wadn't nough Why of a'Sudden here come Calley's little Shimmery Dog up out the Water behind em just a'Yipping and a'Laughing. Then o'Calley give me a Look like he was wanting to tell me Some Thing and I knowed just what it was. So, he said, I pulled his Big o'Pistola out from down my Pants and throwed it way out yonder in the River fars I could get it. Why'd you go and do that Annie said and I said Cause I don't never wanna give it the Chance to Shoot somebody with me a'Standing there a'holding it. And Oh Annie never been more Happy to hear anything in all her Life and give me a'Smile and a Pet on my Cheek. You the Smartest Boy in Town ain't you, she said.

*T*HEN OF A SUDDEN, Papa said, They was a Big BOOM BOOM BOOM on a'Drum come from up yonder in front a'the Alamo where they was getting ready to Hang Some Body. Wonder who it is Annie said and Senyora Garza said I don't know but theys lots to pick from round here if you ask me. And then, he said, we went a'Walking on up there to see for our self and Oh they was People just bout ever wheres you Looked and most of em had they little Son and Daughter

. here come o'Johnny on that Big White
orse just a'Blowing and a'Shimmering
out the Water . . .

147

up on they Shoulder to give em a'Better Look and Oh they was so many Shimmery Horses come to see the Hanging too you could a'give ever one a'o'Genral Houston's Boys a'Horse for Christmas and still had nough left over for all the Little Boys and Girls in Blanco County. Oh and then, Papa said, I looked over there and seen them Seven Old Men a'setting up they Table and Chairs but Annie give me a Poke in my Rib to Look at what she was a'Looking at in sted and what it was, he said, was two men a'Pushing this other Man up the steps a'the Hanging Stand to where they was a'Noose just a'Dangling. Oh that poor Man, Annie said, I wonder what he done in his Life to come to this. Well I can tell you what he done to come to this, a Man behind us said. He Murdered a'Bunch a'good Horses is what. And not only them, the Man's Wife said, but I heared a'couple a'Germans too and some Mexkins. But the Horses was the Main Thing the Man said. Oh and then Annie put her Hand to her mouth and said Oh my Goodness Gracious a'Live cause now we could see who it was they was bout to Hang. And who it was, Papa said, was o'Sheriff Simon Pugh his self. Oh and then, he said, they started tightening the Noose round the o'Sheriff's Neck but of a sudden somebody went to Hollering IT'S HIM IT'S HIM IT'S O'SIN NOMBRE IT'S HIM and me and Annie and ever body else in the World turned and Looked over there and why it was them two Old People Big Nose and Little Ears robbed that Day when I was with em and they was a'Snarling and a'Pointing they Finger at me. THAT'S HIM they hollered THAT'S O'SIN NOMBRE RIGHT THERE THAT'S HIM THAT'S HIM RIGHT THERE O'SIN NOM-BRE THAT'S HIM. Oh and then, Papa said, bout six Men grabbed a'holt a'me and couldn't Annie or o'Fritz neither one get em off. HANG HIM some body hollered. HANG O'SIN NOMBRE. Oh and then, he said, they went to pushing me up the steps to the Hanging Stand and ever body went to Hol-lering HANG HIM HANG HIM HANG HIM but then Somebody hollered STOP IT STOP IT YOU GOD DAM IDJITS STOP IT and Oh, Papa said, it was o'Sheriff Pugh his self a'doing the Hollering and every body got just Quiet as some little o'Mouse. Then o'Pugh give Annie a'Look like he was remember-ing he still owed her a'Favor from that Time at the Guadaloop River when we found him tied to that Tree with his o'Bare Hiney just a'Shining. What the god dam Hells wrong with you People, he hollered, That ain't o'Sin Nom-bre. I'm the only one ever seen o'Sin Nombre in his Face and that ain't him. Then one a'them Men a'holding me went to rubbing round all over me and said Well this Fella here ain't even got a Gun on him. I don't reckon o'Sin Nombre'd go any wheres without his Pistol in his Pants would he. I told you, Sheriff Pugh hollered, I told you that ain't him. Then, Papa said, Annie give o'Pugh a'little smile to say Thank You for returning the Favor and he give her a'little Nod back I reckon cause he couldn't work up a'Smile at a'Time like this. Then them two Men stepped him over on top a'the Trap Door and one of em said You got anything you wanna say here at the End and o'Sheriff Pugh said No I can't think a'nothing Maybe just give me a'minute or two to Think bout it but them two didn't see nothing Funny bout it and dropped the Trap Door out from under him and his o'Neck went POP and he Let go a'little Toot PUTTA-PUTTA-PUTTA when he hit the End a'his Rope. And Oh ever body just stood there like Froze Ice cause they never seen or heared nothing like it but may be oncet or twiced in all they whole Life, Papa said. All cep o'Fritz who just couldn't help his self and went Heh Heh Heh.

*A*ND THEN, Papa said, I looked over there to where them Seven Old Men had they Little Table and Chairs set up and o'Shimmery Sheriff Pugh was already a'setting down to count out his Black and White Dominoes but it didn't Look like it was going too Good for him when it come to all the Black ones he was a'getting but then, he said, why here come o'Johnny just a'Shimmering up to the Table and started Arguing with em and then here in a minute why them Old Men took a'couple a'his Black Dominoes back and gave him a'couple a'White Ones in they Place cause a'Some Thing Good o'Johnny tole em bout his Big Brother. But, Papa said, We didn't stay long nough to see how it finally come out for o'Sheriff Pugh in the End.

*W*E BETTER GET ON HOME, Papa said, we still got Us some Graves to dig. But of a'Sudden, he said, Annie give out a'Holler and went a'Running over there to where Mister and Miz Choat was just now coming up in they Wagon with o'Marcellus and Bird a'riding in the Back. Lord we been Worried bout yall Miz Choat said.

149

I'd a'thought Mister Bird here'd a'tole you we was all right I said then hefted the Little Fella up to me and give him a'Hug. He didn't know if you was all right or not Marcellus said. Well I'd a'thought o'Jeffey'd a'tole him, Papa said. She didn't know neither, he said. O'Jeffey can tell you What Direction things is a'going in but can't hardly No Body tell you How they finally gonna come out in the End. Who's them other two People wrapped up there in the Cart, Mister Choat said, I know that one there is o'Calley cause I can see his Spurs is still on him. Annie told em the other two was Pela Rosa and that poor o'Blind Panther used to be Little Missey's Good Friend. Don't matter a'Lick who they are, Mister Choat said, We always got Room for Man or Beast in our Grave Yard. Glad to have em. Yes Sir, Miz Choat said, they always Welcome at our Place ain't they. So, Papa said, me and Mister Choat and o'Marcellus lifted Calley and Pela and that o'Blind Panther up out the Donkey Cart and loaded em in the Back a'Mister and Miz Choat's Wagon then scooted em over a'little to make room for ever body else had to ride back there. Then, he said, we all give Senyora Garza a'Hug and a'Gracias and she went on off in her Donkey Cart just when the Sun started a'going down over there behind them Men a'carrying o'Sheriff Pugh's Dead Body down from the Hanging Stand.

And then, Papa said, we turned for Home and a Whole new Life together with o'Calley's Spurs just a'singing a'Happy Little Tune ever step a'the way Ching e Ching e ChingChingChing . . . Ching e Ching e ChingChingChing . . . Ching e Ching e ChingChingChing . . .

And thus ends

THE DEVIL'S FORK

Book Three of The Papa Stories

ACKNOWLEDGMENTS

This is the third and final volume of the Papa Stories. A lot of good friends have come along for the ride from the very beginning, most especially my pals Steve Harrigan, Bill Broyles, and Connie Todd. That's true of other good friends as well: Keith and Pat Carter . . . George and Bonnie Siddons . . . Michael and Elizabeth O'Brien . . . Barbara Morgan . . . Van Ramsey . . . Dyson Lovell . . . and Rolf Larson. Thanks to all of you. And thanks also to my publisher, Dave Hamrick, and my editor, Casey Kittrell, and to all the good folks at the University of Texas Press who made the publishing of these books such a pleasant and congenial journey, most especially Lindsay Starr . . . Lynne Chapman . . . Colleen Devine Ellis . . . Brenda Jo Hoggatt . . . Dawn Bishop . . . and Papa's most special friend, Jan McInroy. Eternal thanks, also, to my treasured assistant, Joe Pat Davis, whose wise counsel and good company were daily pleasures, just as it was when Kate Bowie (now Carruth) and Amanda Buschman (now Utter) were here on a daily basis. Thank you, sir; thank you, ladies. You were—and are—blessings to both Papa and me. A special thanks to Edward Carey for his spunky illustrations; for me, they're an exact fit for the characters and stories. Thank you, Ed.

And, as always, I thank my dear Sally. Her hand is on everything I do—fortunately.

Bill Wittliff
Plum Creek, February 4, 2018